New People in an Old World
(A Collection of Short Stories)

CU00806415

New People in an Old World

(A Collection of Short Stories)

Phyllis M. Jones

Kenwyn Publishers

First impression: 2009

© Phyllis M. Jones

Published by
Kenwyn Publishers
Pen-y-bont, Heol Sylen, Pontyberem
Carmarthenshire, SA15 5NW

ISBN 978-0-9554248-1-6

Printed in Wales by Dinefwr Press, Llandybie

Contents

Acknowledgements

Cornish Review.
Cornish Scene.
Cambrensis.
Llanelli Miscellany.
Department of Extra-mural Studies, Aberystwyth
with the support of the West Wales Association
for the Arts.

Caravans on the Mountain

Even without the straw hat which he wore when weather permitted he should have been painted by Cezanne. His face was lined and burnt by suns of many seasons, it had a Mediterranean quality. He was a peasant with the dignity derived from long family associations with land.

On the Welsh hillside it was haymaking time.

He walked to the top fields through steep, green hedges over the stony track. The stones shone as if they were polished but, as he regarded the bedrock centre of the lane, his eyes grieved.

Each year it affected him more.

It had rained hard during last autumn and winter, rain which had continued through the spring, yet some things were good. There was growth. Growth was strong as if nature was fighting and, as there had been two or three fine days last week, there was a chance to cut some of the grass. One or two fields, at least, could be 'killed'.

He paused to look down over the valley, 'Dhew, walking on this path is like walking over solid rock.' When his breath returned he walked more slowly to the top, his vantage point, Disgwylfa (the look out). Their farm was rightly named. Just below him the farmhouse, cream with red windows, was solid and square and below that, in the valley, lesser buildings took their place in the pattern, a design which was unruly and spreading.

Ty'n y Cwm looked as brash as their new owners in its vivid white snowcem; granite walls out-thrust from some of the other houses. He saw two caravans, large living type caravans, crowding the mountain. Two caravans meant two more families. He liked people well enough in the markets or sales, but his land always stretched to its boundaries in green isolation. Men scarred the land; lorries carrying window frames or doors or carting rubble stirred summer dust and made the tracks bare and brown. There were ragged gaps in hedges where they passed. These were not people who merged into the land.

Year after year his family depended on him for his weather forecasts, seeking still his old wisdom, wisdom which was the accumulation of country lore. For them he had taken his stick and climbed here to the top field where nothing came between him and the smell of the wind. He counted the seven counties, a line of coast from Worm's Head in Gower opposite a rocky line from Carmarthen to Cardigan and, on clear days, beyond. When the green lands between Sylen and Pembroke were sharp and clear and Rhossili seemed close the weather prospects were poor. This evening clouds threaded through an orange sky which likened it to an inland lake, it reflected the sunset. This was ominous and darkened his mind. Prospects were worse than poor. To cut grass or not to cut. Last year there was no second chance. Mostly he took the good with the bad and, as others said, maybe a second bad summer was unlikely. It was the uneasy thought of time, swift passing and short which oppressed him.

Time, progress and change. Not always for the worst he reckoned. Progress was not always destructive. The new milking parlour, for instance. The boys and his wife had laughed at his wonder when the new system was installed. He had crossed the yard a dozen times to watch the creamy flow. It was as close as he would ever be to a miracle. The white, slightly uneven stream of milk seeping through glass tubes; hour glass containers and the maze of smaller tubes until a new sound told them the flow had reached the cooling tank. He realised it was certain the outlay of money, labour and enthusiasm would pay off. The boys would have a new life, a new sophistication which to them might mean more clothes, more cars, more machinery and eventually . . . his mind paused as he considered what else. There was enough stock, enough land. His elder son marvelled with him, not unexpected in a man brought up in an age when a simple cog-wheel was genius. He was less ambitious than the others, only wishing for a good harvest and a bit of a break afterwards and he would be content. David offered a silent prayer at the time when his miracle could not be ruined by storm or drought.

Progress meant also there was less need for him to leave the comfort of a kitchen when nights were cold. It promised a little cosseting. He did not mind the fact that there were fewer chores for him because he knew the family still respected his old wisdom. If he wanted he could go out and always, when the weather was fine, he was there. When there was a decision he made it or had the last word in a family discussion. Like now, about killing the big field. It was his decision.

The two years, eight seasons, rain, cold and rain again seemed a life-time, during which he had passed from enjoying leisure to a state in which he watched his sons go out to milk, almost with envy.

This first week in June had brought a new problem. It was not the weather alone which made his face look thin and strained. Pain . . . not strange to him exactly, he had had his share of broken fingers, broken ribs, sprains, arthritis in his back and hips which had meant a bit of sweat at times, but pain could be sharp without bringing fear. In the beginning this new pain was a rawness inside which he knew was not right. Over the months the rawness developed into a nagging, boring agony. It was a pain he could not escape from and which showed. The family noticed, they wanted him to see a doctor, but just as he could read the skies and know if tomorrow's wind would blow from the north or west or if there would be a frost; just as he happened to be waiting close when the cow was ready to calve, he knew that a doctor would force them to send him to that alien world he had visited often to see sick relatives. And there would be no return.

At times he kept his head low so that the pain would not be obvious on his face. Today at teatime he could not look at a morsel of food, let alone eat.

Yet now, on his high land, it was time to turn his thoughts to the hay. To bring it in or not? And if he decided there was not one of them strong enough to stop him.

*   *   *

The tractor he used was small and now he had made it to the top field he studied the skies as the worn machine went round and round. He smelt the breath of the mountain and heard other tractors whir in unison. He saw the distant coastline marking the Welsh counties, a green and chequered land rising towards the mountains. This year, the orange and brown stripes were seen in greater numbers; many remembered the futile wait for sunny days last year.

The family team work had broken down a bit since last summer, which had meant they were not the first in the field. He had an extra responsibility, like holding a team of lively horses together. Now, in his tractor time-machine, he was driving with rhythm from the edge of the field to the centre. The air had cooled and a wind was curving the branches of the tree-line towards the north-east. It smelt of rain. He had recommended starting against the grain, he had said – 'Time was scarce' – he meant his time. His own pride in his judgement had given way under the certainty that his time might be as short as the three fine-day span they needed to make their hay.

His heart beat in time with the engine, a sound which throbbed across the fields. Overhead the clouds he had expected last evening were passing. Large clouds now were backed by a black, purple fullness in the west. His hope was in the strength of the wind, the faster the clouds moved the quicker the light behind the mauve would gain in strength.

The pain was bad today. He thought of the look on his wife's face this morning but she had not dared question his taking over the 'turning'. All his life the weather had been friend or enemy but just now the chips were down and he knew it. The skies could beat him. Not beat him fairly, but to beat him in the first rounds of the fight. He was alone against weather and time. As the tractor whirred he tried to forget. Rooks played overhead and the small nondescript warblers darted quickly in the foliage near the edge of the woodland. The swallows flew low.

Underneath the long grass, was grass more green? It needed the sun, but without the sun even this cool wind could dry. If the family pulled together and with a bit of luck there was still a hope that by tomorrow the last bales would be under cover.

The wind was less threatening and all seemed well. He was sure that he could hold out until it was finished. His responsibility ended physically when the hay was made, the younger men took over with their complicated tractors and balers and would do the handling. Mentally though, he would be strung taut until the family had settled around the embers of the kitchen fire to discuss the merits of the day's activity.

A cloud passed over the sun and just as half the field was left for the final airing the rain poured on the mown grass.

He stopped the tractor and stared. For a few hours today he had thought God was on his side. He had muttered at one time out loud, 'Thank you, God, for giving me today.' Not that he was religious, but no one could work with life and growing and not feel that somebody, somehow, had a part in the pattern of things. And now God had let him down. For a moment he thought this and then his whole mind was set on winning. The shower passed as quickly as it came. He stopped the tractor and walked slowly over the lines of the crop to the thickest part in the middle. He stared down at the beads of water which lay along the grass. He put his hand carefully into the mound to see how far the moisture had penetrated; then his frail body bent and he gathered the almost dry grass and turned it with his arms. Six acres of long lines and the futile thought crossed his mind of repeating his movement until the whole lot had been twined towards the air. He felt that it needed his own personal strength and warmth to defeat the elements.

A shaft of sunlight warmed the back of his neck and he recalled that the longest day was still to come. The daylight hours were long enough and much could change in one hour. This thought took hold . . . so much could change in an hour . . . a day. He looked at the thick, green grass growing inside the hedges and the thin, rustling stalks, yellowed on the land. He felt in his pocket for his cigarettes and the lighter. Not his old favourite but the one they had bought him from the supermarket. A flimsy trifle, yet the flame burned bright, even in the wind. He liked the smallness, the expendability appealed which was strange, the plastic material was not really to his taste, but, holding the lighter in his hand and seeing the flame, bright and transient, was having a grasp on life. He thought it was worth taking the tractor back and having something to eat in the house. He could drink some tea, strong and sweet. However, to get to the house and back would take time which was precious. His energy must be spent here on this land.

How long he worked was never known but two hours later they found him, a frail dark figure crumpled against the thick strength of his tractor. Half a cigarette had spent itself into the ground which was now dampening from the evening dew. His lighter lay beside him, a small cheap object . . . expendable.

The sky had cleared and the hay lay in heaps as if a spirit in the wind had dried it.

After the Sale

I looked over Bryndu, down across the *brwyn* where smoke was rising still from the smouldering peat. From patches, all over, smoke rose and where the peat was deep, the strips in the moorland glowed like lava, brilliant and sinister. Only black, buckled sheets of galvanised iron piled where there had been the barn. I wondered about the white owl. It was seven years old they said, the same age as myself. Tom's oak chair from which he watched the valley on so many evenings was a scorched skeleton.

*   *   *

It was during the heat wave after the sale. I rode Silva, not knowing which way was best. Smoke was curling from hidden fires all over. The siren from the fire engine sounded near the top of the mountain, so I chose the lower path. Silva was edgy enough as it was. Priorities change and it was the area around Llwyn Onn which became the centre of a red, flaming, hissing and steaming battle. A fire in the middle of a ring of rushes.

Silva wheeled towards Tŷ Gwyn. He galloped, without my touching him, through the break of trees, down our track and his home. He spent that night in a stable. In a bath of sweat and still shivering from his equine fears. I stayed at the farm with my grandparents. None of us slept. The threat had been too close.

*   *   *

Woodlands dark green. The leaves on branches were weighted by mist. Even the trees drooped. Between parts of the farm track, water lay, thickened by mud into a slippery paste.

13

Already strangers moved over the land. Singly or in groups they stared at and prodded the remaining cattle and ewes; studied tools in the shed, wheelbarrows, the heavy roller . . . anything. They looked long at the *gambo*, at the weather-bleached and beautiful oak boards which had carried thousands of bales. They studied with serious fingers obsolete rakes with wooden teeth. They looked at rusted wheels. Intense interest was shown in the trap once used to take Tom's father and his family to the market . . . years and years long past. With ease I imagined this. I had been told so many times. Tom had described it to us himself, how the mare had bolted at the turning by Bryndu when he was a boy and how the trap had overturned. He was thrown out and everyone thought that was it.

Our two families had been neighbours for years. We shared family lore as much as we shared the labour, events and emotions of the two farms.

Potential bidders were oblivious to the soft, sheeting rain which developed from the mist when dark clouds lowered. Drops beat on galvanised roofs or on their oiled, much-stained raincoats. Pools spread on spaces between buildings. Many were interested in the tractor. Most of them knew just how much it had been used.

On the day of the sale I ran between our farm and Llwyn Onn. I felt the bristling excitement. At Tŷ Gwyn, when pressed, I sat with our family at the grained table. I ate little, pushing aside my plate of broth and potatoes to pick a few biscuits, before buttoning my coat and running back along our farm road over their track, towards the activity. I rejoined the wolfish group which was widening.

Tom, Llwyn Onn, would have been mad. All this happening on his land without his knowing.

*   *   *

14

Our couch was sheltered and warm. An old byre, once used to rear the one calf in deep litter, was now neglected. Stone steps to its door, worn yet mossy. The old straw and dung which had dried into hard, quite pleasant pats, like tiles, covered the floor. Cobwebs draped like silk over each corner. I squatted near Geraint. We were together always, like brother and sister.

He was silent when I gave out bits of information. How Jimmy Price was after the tractor. I knew because he was running it down as much as he could to the men up by the stock shed. I told Geraint how the English couple who had bought Nan's small holding were after the wooden rakes; how the auctioneer had set up his platform. I grumbled about the way Tŷ Gwyn was crowded out with all the family and that they were all coming over as soon as dinner was cleared and when they had dressed. In spite of his sad silence, I chattered on. 'Ivor was going to do most of the milking that night; Dickie was wearing his best cap.'

Geraint's mind was concentrating on the end of his time at Llwyn Onn . . . 'If I was their son . . .' and his voice reproached the couple who were now united under their granite paving in the churchyard. Geraint was always at the farm, helping Tom. From a young boy he had practically lived there. He might have been a distant relation. I was never sure. We thought of him always as being with the farm.

'I've never seen so many people on the mountain. I haven't had a minute all day. D'you know I haven't taken off my coat . . . not once. Our place is crowded. All of them round the table . . . all day.'

He said, 'I couldn't stand to be near when that hammer bangs out who is to have what. And to know strangers have Llwyn Onn. If I wasn't such a distant relation. The same blood is in me though . . . if I had money . . . if . . . even if . . . well . . . But only someone like me who knows it, who's strong and wanting,

15

should take it on. Anyone, even if they had a million pounds, could never feel for it; and feeling is . . . well, feeling. The same blood and the same land.'

I pulled at his jacket to stop his staring with the black, terrible look in his eye. I said in a low voice, the bright rise of enthusiasm dimmed: 'I asked if I could have had Fan for myself.' Fan was the shiny, warm-bodied bitch, black and white, loving me. Geraint turned with a suspicious interest and when I shook my head and tears burned in my eyes, he gripped my hand.

'See what I mean,' he said.

'Gwyneira told me, Tom had said she could have the rakes. She had her baskets filled with her shopping and couldn't carry them home at the time. She asked for them . . . they were hers . . . for cleaning the paddock at her back. They said no. They were for the sale.'

Geraint said, 'Gwyneira filled baskets of apples for our kegs when we went past her footpath to school.'

'Who else would want them . . . wooden teeth?'

'That English couple,' he spat out the words, 'they'll stick them on their wall.'

I said, 'Look at all that *stife* in the sky.'

'You mean cloud,' Geraint answered.

Together we watched the crowd draw into a dark insect formation around the auctioneer's stage. We saw Jimmy Price, his arms flailing through friends and foe, thrusting elbows and shoulders, using his body to the right and left. Jimmy stood in a direct line from the platform. He was tall enough.

When the auction began Gwyneira was at the front. It seemed to us as if she was pushing her way to the back. She had on a faded brown raincoat and her woollen hat. She clutched her handbag. Farmers around jostled with strangers. Most knew what each other wanted. They could use this occasion to settle the old and not forgotten scores. Most of all they wanted to know who had bought the farm and for how much. It had been taken off the market. Everyone would know by the end of the day.

'If I could have raised a mortgage, I'd buy all the stock.' Geraint was lying flat, looking out of the broken door. His moody face above hunched, supporting shoulders.

'Jimmy Price is still pretending. He's not bidding yet.'

'He'll have that tractor.'

'How d'you know?'

'He's smart enough.' The resignation is Geraint's voice made me sad.

'I shan't marry a farmer.'

Geraint turned towards me, 'You will.' His eyes had a funny, scrutinising look.

I thought, when I knew whether Jimmy had his tractor, or whether Gwyneira managed to get her rakes, I'll find Silva, my white pony. I'll take him up the mountain. Geraint was looking at the old hay piled high in the barn . . . dry like tinder.

He thought how the house was near . . . dangerously near. He said, 'It won't be raining like this always.'

All Dreams Contained

The shortest day has passed and it is the beginning of another year. It is the moment when the world stays on its pivot. The mind in its dark concentration matches the shadow of the night but there is the excitement of a new beginning.

On this Welsh hillside Silwyn yields to the list, the year has its own agenda and it must be followed.

The weight of a woven Welsh blanket brought it to the bedroom floor and cold air awakened him. The heat from the kitchen had been subdued overnight and his blood had not yet generated warmth. No matter, habit had taken over as soon as morning air nudged him into a familiar day. Stairs creaked as he moved down into the kitchen, long woollen stockings hung over the door of the oven and his boots ranged with the others on flagstones near the door. No alarm clock was necessary, no tinny, noisy clock could supersede the slow tick of the grandfather clock which, ever more yellowing, stood against the back wall of the kitchen.

His son, David, did not remember the clock being anywhere else and neither did he, when he considered, had his father. The picture on the face which was that of a squat, thatched cottage was imprinted firmly on Silwyn's mind. David sat on an old milking stool, grained down to its natural sheen which had been brought in to serve out its last usefulness indoors. The old man turned his head slightly to acknowledge his son's presence; small faggots had been piled on to the glow fanned by draught, and other small blocks of wood were ready. Silwyn moved to the table where the mugs and tea bags were left for them and made

18

the tea, and soon the steaming liquid fuelled father and son. No word was spoken, their silent communication was sufficient.

The same pattern each day. Silwyn's frame moved with simple precision though hundreds of calories spent themselves in pure mountain air around the cream haven of the farm. Each movement provided momentum for the next. Together the two men wrapped in their bulky clothes walked towards the yard.

They passed the farm field, the level plain of which led past the back of the house. Silwyn frowned at the deep ruts caused by the tractor, 'We'll never smooth off those marks,' he spoke his first words of the day. David looked at the scoured earth and said, 'I'll put the chains ready when I have the chance.' He knew the sight of those ruts sickened his father and he would fix them. It would be as his father wished.

David never mentioned the word 'machinery' yet it vibrated between them. It was always a point of difference between two dedicated hill farmers; if not machines it was a reminder of another age. At a family conference the subject was bound to be raised and the obvious advantage of mechanical improvements was a threat the father was able to resist. He did this with patriarchal stubbornness making it un-answerable There would follow a spate of remarks against David as other members seized this opportunity to show, as far as they dared, their criticism. Spite was evident in niggling pettiness, 'David would clear that whole patch of woodland if he could gain a few extra bales,' or 'Remember, that's where the holly with all the berries grows,' and 'That would ruin the view of the mountain' – all comments combined in these words, 'David never appreciates our own land.' Once that last remark was underlined with, 'Even in animals, our calves.' Our calves, Silwyn wished he had the words to explain what his animals meant to him. How could they know that I watch the sheen on the coats of the calves and their mothers, or understand the light feeling I have when a calf suckles its mother for the first time; how I am moved when it staggers and falls after stumbling to its knees. But he could not form his thoughts into words.

David had a love-hate relationship with machinery, he had almost as much of an antipathy as had his father, but his objections were diluted. He knew how the tractors and different appendages made light work of the season's programme, silage making for example, his sense of pride was boundless at the sight of the black, shining rows of wrapped mounds of fodder, enough for as many cattle as the land could accommodate; how scrubbed clean were the stalls when the bedding could be scooped out in one metallic action. And there was the miracle of the milking parlour. This last boon had erased the memory, almost, of the wasteful hours spent in childhood, as he sat by the side of a fractious cow, or leant into muddy flanks, drowsy and cold, using hands which worked as if they possessed a separate life, pulling at teats, and the sound of a frothing squirt into pails, already scalded; and the follow-up work, the utensils to be re-scrubbed and sterilised and the sick-making tiredness at the end of the day. Yes, that was a memory which time may have sweetened, yet not quite enough to erase the resentment of an exhausted child. Sometimes, however, the thought helped to assuage his boredom.

Milking completed and the daily visit of the milk lorry over, a breakfast was enjoyed by the two men. The morning, now empty, gave a sense of control . . . it was in front of them.

David wished he could also just stand and stare. He watched his father walk over the stony path which led to the top slopes of the farm; his expression softened as he nodded with tolerant affection; he knew how the older man could let a few hours slip past by just looking. Silwyn's strong face had its secret expression but the battered binoculars, the leather coverings worn, stretched the fabric of his coat pocket, proclaimed to any member of the family his intentions. 'His glasses' the only object he would claim as his personal property.

*　　*　　*

The old man could not have found a better vantage point even though this was not the highest level of the mountain. To the north was the Waun which stretched to the foot of the next slope and set in relief the top of the mountain. The Waun was not as dangerous as it had been, but a man had to know his way; he remembered when his father's brother floundered whilst riding his cob home from the market in Llanelli, the cob was never seen again and at the time his uncle had frightened everyone in the farmhouse when he appeared, like an apparition, with mud caked all over him and his face as white as snow. Just now the foliage was bleached by all the winds which blew over Sylen, but in summer it would be blowing with flax. As usual Silwyn settled on an old stone slab to look across the valley. There was more to see in this direction and he always allowed himself time to absorb the scene. From this stone he watched the changing seasons, he felt how the weather would change, he noted the smell from the wind and soil, the feeling in his own joints or bones; he noted small differences in the surrounding holdings which he could report to the family later, across the meal table. He knew by heart all the colours of the world around him and the silhouette of every tree. He forced the family to be aware of his passion and sometimes, with reluctance, they were persuaded, even those who would have escaped, to remain in the home farm. When Silwyn was in a good mood, meal times were lively, his old face would break into chuckles at stories which were told and he would regale them with his own tales of how things were when he was a boy. David at times like this, would lean against his own chair back, beaming with fondness at his father who sat on the the heavy settle, the arm rests of which were worn to the shape of his old hands which smoothed them over and over.

*   *   *

David travelled along the same path just as often; perhaps thinking the same thoughts when he passed the grove beneath the sheltered side of the hill, he might see the holly tree loaded with its vivid berries (when the season was right); it was a matter of course, not interest, when the sparrow hawk soared over the Waun, not even causing him to shorten his stride. He saw and heard without thinking, yet all the time he wished he could watch as his father watched. Silwyn was able to measure time, his work output surpassed any other member of the hillside community, even counting the younger generation in spite of their vitality. Slowly he paced himself and no one could compete with that measured tread.

If it was possible, if David was pragmatic, if he could arrange the thoughts which did pass so rapidly through his mind, he would have admitted to that envy of his father's ability . . . to stand and . . . just look. But for himself, the seasons came and went, marked only by the needs of the animals and the growth around him. Yet . . . he knew he was the farmer . . . blood of my blood.

*   *   *

The farm was his, as much by right of love as his future inheritance and, if ever such thoughts passed, it would be momentarily, to consider how his work was within his self-imposed time limit; to assess the crop, count, to within one or two, the numbers of bales, to judge the texture of the crop, the onset of a storm. All this knowledge was breathed into himself, the problems solved and solutions retained, always the equation served to increase his experience, his unrealised pride, never to be expressed. The words, 'I am the farmer' were written on his soul, they projected that extra, almost maniacal strength and a pride which no work, however harrowing, would diminish.

The family with their energies and words, their increasing social activities, the high life and arrogant disregard for older values of the new generation, never affected him. 'I am the farmer' words felt and never spoken, gave him his own value.

Only Silwyn, doyen, the father was his equal, his superior, the one man with whom he felt an affinity.

Security was assured while the heads of the family were strong, the balance was maintained, he could do as he wished. David's material wealth was to be counted, contained in a small box hidden under his bed. It was all he needed.

Things were better now that he himself was older and knew, at least in his father's eyes, he was treated as a man. At the family gatherings the strong table was laden with food augmented by fruits of each season's harvest: mushrooms, blackberries, potatoes and beef; the ritual killing of a pig and always the daughters came from their own homes to help, priority was always given to the home farm. All were equal in their deference to the matriarch, Elizabeth. No scrap of family news escaped her notice. David accepted his position as the chief provider without any resentment against the powerful personalities above him.

Each hour since he had been born was spent in absorbing the life of his farm. His childhood's passing sights or sounds or smells without conscious effort, had steeped him in the atmosphere of the mountain. His waking moments, in the cot in his parents' room, in the kitchen and outside, in a pram or crawling along the flagged paths or walking around the calves' bier in the cowshed, in the yard when the herd had gathered, morning and evening, the sounds, milk jetting into a pail, lowing of cows the seasonal highlights, first swallows nesting, their twittering, their lining up prior to autumnal flight, the sound of a cuckoo on a magical day in May . . . and now the sight of milk flowing through glass tubes and the sound of a tractor, the strong dry smell of made hay. This constant colour made a backdrop to his life and had been absorbed. It was there, part of himself. The backdrop might have been as colourless as the greyest mountain drizzle. He belonged, he was no summer visitor as were the swallow and the cuckoo, nor the daughters who came and went. He was the one who heard and was part of the night sounds of the family, gentle snoring; hot words as siblings wrangled. All this was his world, and had been the stage for his own act in his own world.

Every other person in his life, mother, father, brothers and sisters were kept together by words. David listened to the opinions and arguments, sometimes dreams, and they merged with the other sounds in his life. His own words were held inside him, locked in an echoing chamber which separated him from the rest. It was right that it should be so. The others had escaped the tyranny of the family while he had accepted it. Each in his different way had established a life of his own, created a little dynasty and managed to maintain a filial self-interest. They were reaching into other worlds, a caravan by the sea, a convenient retreat at times; meals in a restaurant, shopping trips, holidays overseas, they were reaching into that other world as they kept their grip on their own.

*   *   *

The sun comes in its season.

David was aware of the power in the new tractor. Each time it thrust itself along the length of the main field he felt the clean, sweeping cut of the blades as if it were an extra effort of his own body. The sensuous movements of his arms which guided and his legs which controlled the power brought that perfect warmth of well-being.

It was not too hot that evening inside the cabin of his machine; the sun had dipped below the Prescelly Hills and been robbed of its maximum heat; there was enough daylight left to finish the particular task he had set himself and soon, he knew so well, after all these years of working alone in the fields, the earth would breathe out the smells of evening, the crushed grass, the fragrance of May blossom, the stronger farmyard smell wafting down from the hill; the noise of the engine would drown the rustles, the flight of a birds' wing, the snap of twigs sounding on the edge of the woodland, but he knew the sounds were there. He heard, even if it was only in his mind, the softer whir of the light flailing machine his father was using in the top fields. For one moment as the sounds of the machines merged to any distant observer of the whole scene, his mind merged with his father's. Two minds which had joined into one sequence of practical plans, dreams and utter physical dedication into the soul of their land.

He did not realise there was a smile on his browned, steadfast face and could never have appreciated just how perfect was the match of his thoughts to the texture of the evening. It was almost midsummer, the light on this evening would never fade.

Courting

Wind . . . cold from the north-west. The last of the leaves whirled along the small road and the corner had changed overnight into a winter stage. I saw the young couple as they sheltered against the hedge. His arm had moved away from her shoulder and was now flung across her body . . . a gesture of protection.

It was the first glimpse of the couple and it touched me.

A boy with his arm across his girl's shoulders, walking on a country road. It was important on that near winter's day to fix the moment in my mind. I could not find the word, bucolic was patronising and young love obvious. Besides, it was only a normal boy and girl courting scene made colourful against a background of stark branches and gutters filled because of the gale's mischief. Just because it was 'old fashioned' . . . Yes . . . that was the word. When I recognised the boy I understood. He was old fashioned. He worked in the local colliery and I had one or two conversations with him when he came into the Medical Centre. Always the men made an effort to be polite when they wanted advice or treatment in the Centre, but this boy had an innocence and eagerness in his manner which set him a little apart. His brown hair curled round his country face and his eyes looked into mine with frankness. The men teased him, but I noticed the rough working colliers had a tenderness in their voices.

Bryn was a face-worker and valued by management for his endurance and humour and that so-easily-taken-for-granted courage. It was a fact that he and his fellow team members slipped in the Medical Room for minor treatment just to get their name on the official dressing list. Custom and practice! And we all contributed to this not-quite-innocent deception – even when Will, the Under-Manager, entered the Medical Room at the same time; inevitable play-acting banter covered the awkward moment. On the day I remembered, Bryn and Vivian sat on my two green-leathered chairs. Vivian was needing a finger plaster and I was about to place it. He brought a breath of the November day with him. His hair was ruffled and his coat was spattered from one of those blustering showers. Bryn said to me, 'The usual.' I nodded, and he knew I'd write his name on the list. He turned to Vivian, 'Watch those hands, lad. Keep those courting fingers soft.' No offence meant and none taken. Vivian blushed and laughed. Vivian knew they were on his side. He'd laugh at their jokes and go on his way . . . through the door and to the Baths.

*   *   *

Just now my car edged past the couple. I raised my hand and the boy waved back. His warm smile showed he knew me.

I worked amongst the colliers. At one time there were as many as eighteen hundred employed in the Complex. The number might induce a bland generalisation of faces, but not for me. There might be a hundred Bryns or even a few Vivians, but the always-changing work scene, the humour and danger, as well as the size and shape, age and ancient life of the fossils kept the scene alive and there was real interest in this working background. Colliers are often worn out, injured or frightened, but hardly ever bored.

*   *   *

May time brought its own scenario of plump buds and blackthorn. And the air was scented as I drove down the mountain road. Gwendraeth folk have these moments in abundance because there is such a variety of weather and there are sharp changes of seasons. I looked about me as I steered around this corner. It was my habit of late. Yes . . . he was there. A country swain and his lass and they were courting. The young colliery worker and his girlfriend leant over the gate. It was one of the few remaining wooden gates and was well-seasoned . . . timeless. Their heads were together and their shoulders touched. If they heard my passing car they showed no sign.

I did not realise the speed of the car had lessened as I drove back to my home, relaxation had loosened all the muscles on my body and the pressure on the accelerator pedal was reduced. I tried to imagine their conversation . . . sweet nonsense or promises as they forged their dreams into plans.

*　　*　　*

It was September. This morning as I passed Vivian's corner I noticed the leaves were crisping and the air had that bite which is a tonic after a long warm summer's day.

End of the shift in the colliery, the passages and corridors were buzzing with voices and sounding with heavy boots on moving feet and, because it was payday, there were the usual cameos. Two men engaged in a private transaction as a few notes were exchanged. Several men perusing, carefully, their payslips and some were going back to the glass office windows to check figures. A few afternoon shift men were already squatting with their 'Collier's Crouch' along the passage outside the Medical Centre. They filled the extra time they had allotted themselves with argument and repartee; much gossip and the occasional political homily. Entering the Baths was delayed until the day shift had gone through and some were clutching carrier bags full of the fresh produce an enterprising local farmer was selling, at

28

his below supermarket prices, from his van at the colliery gates. Fridays was a day when all aspects of life in our colliery came together and were found to be good.

Bryn was later than usual because it was payday and there was no point in his coming up early. He was there when Vivian came in with the bright look of someone who has not yet worked his shift.

'Well boy . . . you're not on the married man's shift yet, are you? What about your courting?' Vivian turned his head and laughed, then, with a cheeky, just-watch-this-gesture, he produced one of those traditional wedding-cake boxes from his jacket pocket and handed it to me. Now his expression was courteous and his eyes triumphant; there was joy, hope and his certainty of my congratulation in his look.

Of course I held out my arms instinctively. I wanted to hug him. Bryn was the surprise of the day. He turned from the door which he had opened and moved towards us. He held out his hand and gripped Vivian's. I noticed the rough strength of the hand and the little blue marks . . . coal dust accumulates so easily in the multiple cuts and scratches and leaves a permanent tattoo. I noticed also the soft, remembering look in Bryn's eyes and that wonderful smile of Vivian's. 'Good luck and all the best, lad,' Bryn said.

*   *   *

My corner near the entrance of the mountain road was set for winter. Spring, summer . . . autumn, I suppose, is the most spectacular, but winter, as today, with sombre and sculptured trees making patterns on a silver sliver of sky promises that soon we will experience those muffled days when each branch will carry its quota of snow and the whole world is muted. I never minded the weather. What I minded was the rationing of daylight which made routine chores a challenge.

Each tree made its own pattern. I noticed one branch had splintered away after the October gales. It was hanging, poised, to drop into the mulch piled in the ditch. My mind moved to the thought of that branch hardening into stone after millions of fossilising years. The colliers told me their stories of sudden lethal falls when such a branch was loosened after vibration from use of picks and, in modern times, from the relentless cutters. These petrified pieces of tree trunks were uniform in shape and a ridged surface proved its original design. Men would bring me shining anthracite imprinted with a fern or flower. The mystery of time and the economy of nature. Nothing is ever lost. I thought of the Mare's Tail which was a plague in our gardens . . . an ancient plant with roots nearly ten feet long. I thought of the mystery and organic chemistry and marvelled at the depth in the world under this mountain where our men still worked.

A car passed the gateway I had named, 'Vivian's'. I smiled as I remembered when I last saw him. He was leaving our colliery with its history of floods and fires and 'blow-outs' and was going to work in a smaller private mine . . . 'For safety,' he explained. Once again it was Friday in the Medical Centre with the end-of-the-shift rush. Bryn was there and was accepting Vivian's warm thanks and joining in the chorus of good wishes. Bryn's voice was serious, 'I know Colliery has had its ups and downs, but it isn't a bad old place, boy. We know how far we can go with the bosses and that they're on our side.' A Deputy passed through just at that moment and stared at a billet of wood in Bryn's hand which was scarcely hidden under newspaper. 'Mind, it's hard to believe sometimes.'

Vivian laughed. He was basking in their friendship. He accepted being one of this tough family. One man said in a quiet voice, 'Mind, lad . . . they haven't got our Union. Their bosses think profit first and profit last.'

Serious words are remembered afterwards when the mood is not gay.

*　　*　　*

I was to remember those words when Bryn came in at the end of his shift that winter's day. The Centre was empty and he was earlier than usual. There was no gleam of humour in his eyes and his face showed how few working years remained for him. 'I came up to tell you something bad.' The tone of his voice made me go to the treatment chair to sit. I looked at him. 'Vivian was killed yesterday.' I watched Bryn's lips tighten as he gathered control. 'A fall in the district where he worked. An old tree trunk dropping like a slab of concrete.' I remembered the last time we all met. 'I should have stopped the lad. There's no thought of safety in those small mines.' I stood up and placed my hand over the blue criss-crossed hand of Bryn's. Then, together we walked to the solid door to the corridor. Before it closed behind him I heard Bryn say, 'He was such an old fashioned kid.'

One Cockerel's Footstep

At the end of this long, soaked winter, the mud in the lower field became heavier each day. Gwyn felt as if his feet were clamped on to his own land. This afternoon, one boot had been sucked from his foot and, losing balance, he had fallen, sprawled across the black oozing mire. Out loud, to the grouping herd of Jersey cows, he had cursed the poached acres. Fury and frustration caused his voice to rise in a near scream but the large bovine eyes contemplated him until his cries had faded into the dripping hedgerow.

Wet, rain, mud; animals draining his resources and strength. Cold, freezing dawns and every minute of daylight as precious as a summer's day. Even the thought that tonight would be his night of freedom was small comfort at this moment.

Later, inside the house before milking, he sat in dry clothes with his brother and parents. The damp clothes were stretched on chairs before the fire. His mother cut bread with the large butcher's knife, worn thin since her early days of marriage. Benny ate more quickly so that he and his father could start the milking in plenty of time. He knew that Gwyn would do the same for him tomorrow when it was his turn.

The mother's movements were slow. Her legs were swollen and her body was swollen. She had as little gentleness with herself as she had with the rest of the family. 'Mair called today,' she said, 'Gareth is home from hospital. His hernia's been done. But . . .' she added with hard pity for her neighbour, 'He won't do his work for a while.' The father sighed. He glanced through the panelled window. 'It's brightening. The rain has stopped.

One cockerel's footstep every day. Spring will be late . . . but it comes.'

'I've done your boots,' said his mother. Gwyn's boots, polished like old oak, stood side by side near the grandfather clock. The laces criss-crossed like thongs, made their own pattern. He thought, one day a week and I walk with clean boots! He said, 'Thanks, Mam.' He studied the brown shine of leather and wished, like a boy, for the moment when the soft skin would wrap round his feet and all the evening chores would be completed.

At last. The gate at the end of the lane was caught and in the struggle to free it, his suit became stained. Margaret would notice. She would laugh with her particular mocking laughter, call him her farmer's boy and in the bustling room of the The Farrier's Arms she would tease him in front of all those townies.

He could do without The Farrier's Arms. He would like to go straight to the terraced house which was Margaret's since her mother died. He would have liked to go straight to her over-furnished bedroom with its pink lampshades and white fur rugs. There he would drag her straight beside him between the warm coloured sheets which felt so different from those harsher linen ones at home. He would stretch out his body and revel in the luxury under the flower patterned coverlet; his body, every square inch of it aware of the softness and now, most of all, the smoothness of Margaret's skin . . . absolute luxury and the final, dark losing of himself as he sank into her, lost as the mountain whin is lost in the twining foliage on the hills.

Thus, again, he lay in a state of powered peace, resting and complete. Just once a week, with his mother's certain knowledge that such times were necessary in a man's life to keep him fast in the home's circle.

It was over.

He remained still, thinking of the clover scent from her warm, slightly sweating body. 'You remind me of summer,' he said without knowing why. It was true, haymaking time and summer. But she was asleep. The scent did make him remember clover in fields and warm bales of hay. Summer, long days, swift passing weeks of warmth. Because he spoke the words Margaret became more real. She was his warmth, and comfort, through her, like summer, was soon finished. Margaret, confetti and wedding bells?

He pictured all the family wedding groups nailed on the kitchen walls at home. His father, clear face with eyes dark and wide, looking out of the frame into the room which was his life: his mother seemed never to have changed: his sister Dilys whose wedding picture enclosed a whole family of brothers from the next farm. His sister Jane being married in a blue suit cut rather full over the hips.

Yet the thought of a wife was as strange in his own head as the thought of a holiday in Spain. Marry . . . yes, maybe the daughter of another farmer, someone who would inherit her own acres. But who was there? His eyes, now accustomed to the faint street lighting, fell on the thick window recess. A good solid wall which made him think of the strong stalls in the stable, smell of hay and the champ, champ, comforting sound of healthy animals behind the closed stable doors. He turned his head towards Margaret. Even in her sleep, she sensed he was looking at her. She sighed and her hand reached out across his chest, grasping his forearm. For a woman, not a country woman, the grip was firm. He brought his mind back to this moment, the present. Himself lying between sleep and acute awareness of now, tomorrow and tomorrow with only yesterday pushed into a drab past. The woman's fingers pressed into his hard muscles. He did not take his eyes from her face, he concentrated only on the imprisoning fingers. Her skin was colourless as she slept and her mouth had lost its mocking tightness. Not once, since the night, two years ago, when he had first walked with her from the pub to her home had he ever thought she might love him. What was love?

Somehow, through the yellow glow outside, he was conscious of another light, a lessening of dark. One cockerel's step in time earlier than yesterday. He moved his arm closer to himself, away from the reach of the woman. Was love gratitude for this renewal of energy, the urge directed forwards?

Tomorrow, after milking, he must mend the gap in the field at the top of the Bryn. He would cut some of the trash, bind some of the branches more tightly and put some strands of barbed wire. Much as he hated the stuff there was nothing like it to keep in the stock. And there was the low, hung gate he knew he must mend.

Teilwng Celyn

There was a moment which must have been the beginning.

The colour of the gelding, Teilwng Celyn (The Worthy Holly), wine red under a gloss of white, emphasised the warmth of the animal beneath me. It was a warmth which matched his strength and speed, it suited my mood, exhilaration. I knew I was meant to be here at this moment as the wind crossed from Cardigan towards Gower. I swayed in the wind as it changed direction or power, it was as though I was a reed or a tuft of grass. The ride outwards was a ride into sunlight and sky.

We came to Ynysteddfyn. The walls of the farm outbuildings sheltered an award-winning herd of Welsh Blacks, cows with their calves, which had been herded by Joseph in preparation to a change of pasture. Now he and his brother rested against the pile of grass already cut for silage; they waved as we passed. From their expressions we were their sign that summer had begun. We were as reliable as the cuckoo – the season had begun and we were welcome.

As always on Celyn I felt light. It was as if I had receded into the landscape and was without substance. One moment out of time when there was no rancour, no envies, no hopes, no loves. I was reduced to an element which moved in unison with my horse across a Welsh hill.

Ian, a farmer neighbour, was ahead on the narrow road. He rode his mare and led a pretty, coppery chestnut which carried his niece. The small girl sat as straight as a stick on Geitha. It was her first long ride and her face was intent as she concentrated. Ian's nephew, Peter, was beside me just now and I thought how he had changed during the time I had known him. I have no children, I have no idea how they are or how much they are expected to change . . . but he was different. Peter had been so nervous when I knew him first, an elfin child. There had been a curious look in his eyes which seemed as if he was assessing me and finding me wanting . . . so I thought. It was probably his native distrust in strangers. I was a stranger at that time. I was wary also. And if I had thought, a bit frightened. The hard hilly world where the foliage was burnt by wind and sun was so different from the blue memory of Cornwall, which had been my county.

Yet amongst the mountain community these days, I sensed that Peter was the only one who was receptive to my thoughts and was able to respond. I should not have been surprised, but I did wonder at his ability to put most of his ideas into words. I discovered I could talk to him with a candour that is possible between two people who have known each other for ages. I saw him grow, the boy with fair curls who had watched with so much suspicion when I first became part of this farming world. The boy who sat with the cow in the byres; who knew the dates they were to calve, not only because he was the one who kept the records but because he had an empathy with the animals which could never be learnt from books. He was the boy who knew the names of each beast and sensed their needs. He had shared, at times suffered, the rigours of farm life and had not sacrificed his essential gentleness. He was able to add his own intelligence to the family resources, to temper native instincts and cunning. He gained their trust. I could see that whenever I visited. Through him I knew I was drawing closer to the secret, wet mountain land. At this moment he was riding my strong-willed mare, Honey, who subordinated herself only to Celyn, but allowed those she had to depend on to ride her.

Riding with my friends was a kind of sharing for me. I know we were an oddly assorted group, but there was a thread which tied us and distanced us from those around us. A bond, invisible, of loyalty. Our horses that breathed their instincts through shining coats echoed and emphasised this strange and yet so natural a phenomenon.

Clear sunlight, a view of seven counties on an evening like this evening and the ecstasy of movement.

Celyn stretched his glossy roan forelegs and trotted. I was safe in the knowledge that he would not gallop away from equine company and I allowed myself to move with him. Honey kept pace, stride for stride, and I looked into Peter's eyes and laughed. We veered on to the grass verge and thudded past Ian and his little niece. Ian smiled, his black eyes bright like anthracite. I knew him so well already. He could not justify a landworker's guilt which he felt if he wasted hours of daylight. It was as if Nature would rebel against constant restraints as soon as his back was turned. If I thought he would not look blank I might have said 'It's all right . . . life does have compensations. Enjoy yourself. This isn't exactly a crime.' I knew it was a fear of ridicule from his peers. Riding for pleasure was not done in the real world. He was uneasy. He could not throw off his sense of guilt.

At least he kept his kinship, his affinity with animals and this knowledge extended to an understanding, if not a passion, for horses. He could not appreciate the nervous energy of the animal – it was too sensitive for him. Cattle with their bovine acceptance could be controlled. At times he saw how Peter drew animals to him with so much ease and he wondered why there was that sense of irritation, and if his thoughts could be analysed, he would have recognised envy. Yet who was he to resent his congenial nephew who helped the family so much with their animals?

I sang as I abandoned myself to a wildness of movement. Ian could never sing . . . not out loud. His pleasures had to be contained. All emotions must be suppressed and he could never show gentleness or warmth like his nephew. At times I wondered, when I saw his thick muscles, so solid in his body, if he was aware of his strength. It was a positive thing, as with an athlete without the finesse. It showed in his balance as he sat on his horse and the balance of the animal he rode. He could absorb benefits as well as buffeting from Nature. When he looked across the stony fields towards Rhossili and in the opposite direction towards Cardiganshire his face expressed a pride of ownership. There were mountains, hedges, fields and a coastline as far as he could see, but he was interested more in the men who were working on a tractor that had dragged the harrowing chain over the field. The scene in the foreground obliterated sky and space. He saw his neighbours working, saw and understood what they were doing and he admired the herd of cows with their young calves in a field next to them. He looked towards Peter, 'They look well.' Peter responded, 'The cow with the small calf is like Beth at home.' Together they studied the herd. The farmers turned and waved. These men knew Ian from his market days, they took their friends as they found.

I wished I could tease him, make him laugh. He sat consciously erect in the saddle. Peter rode Honey close to Celyn and said, 'Just look at his expression.' I smiled and faced the contemplative eyes of the farmers, I could understand. It was blatant and although I could dismiss their suspicions with scorn I would not blame them. This was a different culture, perhaps in future they would learn of a friendship, even between men and women, which could be innocent.

I was a widow and lived in the smallholding with the twin sister of my late husband who came down to help with everything after he had died and remained. Probably more for companionship than for help . . . mutual convenience. At home over our own meal table we indulged in gossip as much as anyone. I discussed with shameless interest all the incidents and relations in the lives of my neighbours and I should know better.

Some things were as good as meat and drink. A period of silence told me it was time to say something.

'They . . . the horses, go better in company.'

'And so do we,' Peter added.

Marie turned round and beamed, her riding hat hid most of her face, she was like a little Cheshire cat. We quickened the horses into a fast trot to please her. Marie's pony kept closely to Brownie on the leading line. Ian was careful with her. He never disguised his liking for children, and they took advantage of this, asking for a ride on the nearest farm pony which meant an interruption to the evening's milking, a fact which would cause annoyance to most, yet he complied with a shrug of his shoulders.

We reached the bridge over the small river. On the sidetracks the grass was green and lush; in a field of a newcomer to the area, a herd of Nubian goats grouped like white scraps of paper, patterned the meadow. The slope on this hill was fixed in the memory of our horses, a place associated with abandonment and pleasure, their pace became faster.

Outside in the yard-cum-car park of the inn, Ian held the reins of his horse and Marie's pony; Peter held Honey's head. She was quite enough of a handful on her own. I was delegated to go inside to the bar for our drinks. The landlord smiled from behind the shining counter. His voice welcomed with warmth which made up for a sudden shyness when I was conscious of the heavy riding clothes which had been necessary for me to wear for the ride. Amongst all these townies with smart dresses and high heels and loud voices I tried to be casual.

'Ah . . . so you've made it through the winter. I bet it was good across the mountain. The usual?'

I nodded, he had eased the tension. Someone opened a door for me when I went out with my laden tray. The first of the year. How long I hoped we could continue. We lingered and chatted as we drank. Celyn and Honey stood side by side, relaxed as the evening sun picked up the sheen on their manes and coats. Cars drew up in the car park and people looked with approval. This was 'atmosphere'. For this they had driven miles and would spend money.

Ian lifted Marie and sat her on Celyn's back. The roan, I could see, was aware of the child who was fastening her hands through the thick hair of his mane. If a horse could smile I am certain Celyn smiled.

*　　*　　*

Weeks passed and evenings lengthened and warmed. Each ride differed from another. There were different companions, variation of clouds, the changing colours in the hedges and the weather. This evening my sister's daughter rode Honey. For once I was less of an outsider. I could see Jane was puzzled at the easy communication between Ian and myself. She perceived only the outward crust of that same communication and it was plain she thought it much easier than it was. She appreciated the horses more than the rough farmer but her experience had been confined to the hiring of a horse and lessons in an urban riding school. There was a lack of elegance in this present group and she showed her disapproval too well.

Men were working on the fields next to the Welsh Black's farm. A tractor moved inside the hedge by the road and Brownie, Ian's mare, gained some of her rein from her rider's hand and leapt forward. Both rider and mount had been lulled into a drowsy content by the warmth and smells of the evening. Ian, whose first instinct was to stop his mare and then to ride like some dimly imagined vision of a centaur, jabbed at Brownie's mouth. The mare's head jerked backwards and she cavorted sideways. Ian's back became straighter and his whip cut into Brownie's side. Unnecessary force which jarred our senses.

Jane turned to me, 'Did you see that, Pat? He's not fit to be on that mare.' To Ian she cried, 'Can't you ride her without all those dramatics? You'll ruin her mouth.' I had seen this incident and taken in all the details. It was a small cameo felt as if through antennae rather than witnessed. I dismissed it from my mind because I did not want it to have happened, but Jane's words made it real. I traced my fingers through the black mane on Celyn and pressed myself more firmly into his saddle. I saw Ian's expression when he turned towards me and saw the mixture of surprise, pride and shame on his face. And I looked away from him. I kept my eyes on Celyn's neck, red, strawberry roan was a good description. It was like a layer of copper under silver.

'He'd never ride a horse of mine,' Jane said. I agreed with her so much, I told myself I would never trust him with Celyn. Jane's comment echoed my own anger, no, amended, self-accusation, discomfiture. Even if I explained I knew the difficulty a stranger would have to accept the rural, basic attitude towards animals. If I could talk with Ian I might have explained all this. As it was . . .! I wished Peter were here this evening. Jane would have seen the other side. He might have shown how there was a sensitivity between man and animal. How thoughts, fears, pleasures might be absorbed through the skin. That there was an explanation, an understanding of such reaction. These things could not be learnt in a riding school. Mellow companionship was spoilt by uneasiness.

On the way home, however, we were brightened by our favourite tipple and rode with confidence on horses who picked up all favourable vibrations and extended their paces with extra freedom.

That night rough patches of mountain were alive with field fares who picked and grazed before wheeling in cloudy united swirls from one area to another. Supercilious Jane was laughing. She rode beside Ian and the two broke into a canter ahead of

Celyn and myself. I held Celyn back with difficulty because, resentful at his restraint, he showed it by bucking. Two or three or four times he arched into the air and on each landing strained forward. I was pleased at the breaking down of what could have been a permanent barrier, class and temperament, between Jane and Ian, that I felt relaxed enough to enjoy a smattering of danger. The last part of our journey was down a steep country road and was when I was alone with Jane. We both sang. Jane's voice rang with an unusual inhibition. I sang my familiar song . . . Celyn's song . . . 'I am the Lord of the Dance, said he'. The pitch of the hill proved no problem for the strong legs of Welsh cobs. I revelled in the warm, strong back of the animal, the familiar exercise, 'Dance, dance, wherever you may be . . .' Jane's face when she turned towards me was young and excited.

*　　*　　*

Kate had a salad with cold meat and new potatoes ready. She bustled round the kitchen to make her point. 'You're late this evening.' She kept the sharpness out of her tone because of Jane, but I felt the accusation. 'There were a few odd things to do outside.' I used the time I spent at the sink washing my hands to compose myself and at last we sat around the table. Jane had so much to say that the silence between Kate and myself was not noticed. In the midst of her chatter I heard her say, 'Ian's rather sweet, isn't he?' Kate drew in a deep breath and her thin chest seemed to hold it for a long while before she let out, well, it sounded a mixture of a sigh and a hard, difficult breath. 'Not you too.' She rose and went to pour more water from the kettle into the teapot. 'Hardly sweet,' I replied, wondering and resenting the fact she had changed her opinion.

*　　*　　*

Days reached the month which was warm for riding so we chose to set out at the beginning of the evening. The flies, drawn by the warmth of the animals irritated our horses which spoilt part of the enjoyment. I flicked my whip above Celyn's head to whisk away the vicious insects. He accepted this office as his due. Never any appreciation! Clouds hovered softly still as if their purpose was to decorate the pale blueness of sky. Shorn sheep slept or moved slowly on pasture which was the colour of baked bread. Soon the last of the heat would be tempered by a fresh quickening of air. We all knew the pattern.

This evening Menna was in the party. She rode the dun gelding which she kept at Ian's farm. Celyn hated Sunny and the antipathy was mutual. This was our reason for riding some distance from each other. Menna's husband had gone to school with Ian so there was a background of childhood memories. Lessons, tears, slaps which could not be forgotten. Between those two an older loyalty was to be respected. In Menna's company I heard my voice become more English, even to my own ears it sounded strident. Menna was the most recent member of the group but she was part of her husband who was part of Ian's past. She assumed her seniority with relish.

Tonight, and not for the first time, I wished Peter rode with us. He would have noticed a lack of balance in the conversation and would have ridden near me. I should be ashamed of myself, a woman of my age needing such a young boy to give confidence. I pictured the look he would have given me. His young eyes would be mocking and sympathetic. How perceptive he was for his age. I began to see more plainly that he was a natural bridge between Ian and myself, the professional farmer and someone almost civilised. Peter and the horses made the group authentic. It was a little more than that, the ride was important. I told myself this many times . . . but it was.

I could not help watching Menna. The girl was not an experienced rider but she had the confidence of a beginner. Her

44

flamboyance encouraged Ian who was easily induced to show off; she waved her whip so that it whistled enough to encourage Sunny, young enough to respond, to canter, which soon developed into a gallop. Ian dug his heels in, gathered his reins and soon they were racing on the mountain road. No attempt was made to guide the mounts on to the grass verge. As if to emphasize this I held back my frustrated Celyn and moved over to the grass. The roan, once again, set alight by the movement of the others, bucked and strained at his bridle. The action seemed more dangerous than it was. I shouted at them. Ian stopped and looked back. Menna also stopped. Her look towards me was as scornful as her voice.

'Patricia's Celyn is too much of a handful for her.'

'Steady him up. Keep on the verge,' Ian warned, he was thinking of Brownie who was strutting with as much puffed up pride as Ian would have strutted if he had four feet. I held Celyn and tried to ignore the heat in my cheeks and a stinging in my eyes, 'Galloping on roads is not my style. I like to be in control.' Menna was ahead of Ian. She looked strong and vital. She held her horse with impatience. Ian looked back to me then turned his mare forward, 'Besides . . . I consider Celyn's legs.' My voice was directed towards Ian's back. The sound might have been lost in the soft rustle of a breeze. I stroked Celyn's vibrant, silken neck. I watched the two ride ahead. There was only a belief in my maturity to console myself. I'll never let Ian ride Celyn, I determined.

That night, after leaving the others at the entrance of Tal y Garn, I rode down our hill. Hearing a cry, my attention was drawn by a sparrow hawk. So high and lonely. It hovered overhead as if propped up by the evening air. I knew it would return to its nest between the top foliage of an oak and an ash. I discovered its haunt last autumn whilst picking mushrooms.

Kate would be listening for the sound of hooves on our return. Together we would complete the evening chores with pleasure and I would appreciate being with 'one of my own' as my mother would have said. I had such energy after these ride-outs. Kate knew, I knew, everyone knew . . . or they should . . . that the ride meant companionship, the associated convenience and pleasure in managing the horses. And for safety reasons too, as explained so often to Kate. She answered most times, 'I don't want any excuses.' Kate understood she was welcome to join the party in the groups who came in cars and met us at the Waun Wyllt. She did this once after we had finished the haymaking and there was a party. She felt, she explained, 'a little bit lost and a bit too middle class.' She added, 'You'd say that too if you were honest.'

For a while Menna continued as a regular in our mountain team. Sometimes she and I went on our own. On these occasions we were able to share the pleasure; to exclaim or discuss scenery or incidents if any occurred. Most often we were the uneasy trio and I was alienated. Only on holidays and in the long summer evenings when the 'children', who were now teenagers, came was there a return of the original atmosphere.

It was one rare moment when I forgot I was a stranger to the area. I had felt so well integrated into the background until Menna arrived.

Menna insisted on remaining with Ian to hold the horses. I felt a different kind of humiliation when I went inside to the bar to bring out the drinks. Once I came out with my laden tray to see Ian riding Celyn. He was showing how he could 'master my gelding'. How he postured in front of Menna. He held the reins tightly and pressed his strong legs into Celyn's side and galloped up the road and back. I remained quiet, but I knew my tenseness must have betrayed my fury. When he returned I took Celyn's reins with a deliberate movement and felt Menna's smile. 'Celyn is a teenager's horse really.' I replied, 'He does need real riding.' I saw the exchange of glances between Ian and Menna, and she said, 'Yes . . . we can see.'

My cheeks burned and my eyes stung. I hoped no tears would form. I recalled the time I had seen them laughing and talking as they stood close together. When I had told myself that the incident meant nothing. Things were happier when the younger generation came. Marie, like Peter, never forgot the first wild and happy rides. They looked upon me still as an instigator of pleasure and respected my ability to turn their somewhat dour uncle into a man who was just a part of our simple pleasure. Marie rode Geitha each time. The girl and the little mare had matured together. When we sipped our lemonade, cider or lager, Geitha nuzzled against Marie's shoulder as they shared a packet of crisps.

*   *   *

I was addicted and the ride-outs were becoming an obsession. If the weather was just a little above storm force and the short expedition became impossible, I longed for those hours on the mountain. The date and the venue were always the same but when evenings became too short we rode in the lunch time. We had to ride in the mornings which meant we missed some of the farm work but often it was better. The car park was deserted and the landlord had more time to talk to us. He had become a friend over the years. But after the middle of December we had to stop . . . our animals took more and more energy and daylight was too precious. Animals were housed against winter weather and had to be fed and watered. Kate was a little resentful at my hours away from work and I could not blame her.

The farmers on the hill were relaxed and friendly now, the suspicious expressions were replaced by smiles. I might have been accepted, almost, I thought. When I held Celyn back, not to be involved in a gallop which, because he was faster and stronger and was bound to get into the lead, meant a bit of a battle, they would shout encouragement. 'Come on . . . you'll be late for dinner.' Stupid things like that. 'You should have had a start.'

Summer, autumn, winter and spring, so the years passed. I appreciated the way the younger group 'minded' me. They trusted me as the animals trusted me. I saw that Ian was trusting me also. We spoke more often. Never a long conversation, but words which augmented the silences. I wished Kate had this same trust. Her smiles were a little glassy at times when I reached home, a smile which does not let one through. The old intimacy that was deeper because of Kate's own relationship with my late, sometimes forgotten husband was renewed only when the long evenings drew us back into comfortable discussions and fussy, feminine mealtimes.

The ride was separate to this life and was in itself a life on its own. On my return I would help Kate with supper, make the last drink before bedtime, whirl through the hundred small, homely tasks and was sure that I could shut out the world. Kate might sulk or become angry when I went out to give Teilwng Celyn a last look or give Honey's chestnut coat an extra polish . . . but we both depended on mutual companionship.

Most times I would lean on the round wall which used to be a rest for the milk churns and look towards the hill . . . thinking my own thoughts. There was the cool wooded evening smell to make me wonder about summer growth, abundant all around and the need to trash and tie back the plants which seemed to grow wild. After spring with young plants, tender and un-obtrusive, we had enjoyed an early summer, with fields, clear cut and beige, stark amongst native foliage. There were days when a warm, brandy scent of hay was heavy. The mares and foals would draw near to the barn to savour this promise of winter fodder.

Honey proved barren, was separate from the brood mares. She assumed an equine status of her own, grazing with Celyn, yet in spring I saw at times a yearning look she gave the foals. We have no right to judge but I reflected that it was her way of expressing a human emotion.

So much work. Kate never said a word against Ian.

Autumn rides when the hedges and trees were yellow tatters and paths which had been hidden by leaves and flowers were exposed, were lonely rides. Now Ian was my one companion. The nieces and nephews, friends and rivals, even Menna, had found other interests.

*   *   *

Peter was engaged. There was a family party because Ian's parents were to celebrate their Golden Wedding and the two events meant a real chance for all the relatives to gather at Tal y Garn. Such a large family, all of them in touch with each other and all connected with the land. They were all drawn back to Tal y Garn, even those who thought they had escaped. Now it was for laughter and a feast, often it was when there was need to help with the hay or to build a path or to see the new tractor. The Mother maintained her tight control with invisible wires.

It was plain to see that Peter's fiancée was overwhelmed at the rustic formality in the gathering. In his grandparents' home Peter had a status she had not noticed before when with his parents. Everyone knew Peter was a favourite. I understood this, there was so much of his grandfather in him, I could relate to the older man, in Peter, there was the same quiet strength and a kind respect for his world. Even when weather was bad or there was a sickness with the animals, he accepted setbacks as if he knew tomorrow would bring something to set the record straight. A new calf or one of those perfect Sylen days, clear and pure. The young girl was quiet when voices rose and fell around her and were lost in the hub of the family circle. I guessed she would have preferred a disco.

Kate and I came as Ian's guests. We sat with the doyens. Amidst his family Ian remained just as silent but, as he had the authority which belongs to the instigator of all the activity at the farm (provided it was approved of by the mother), he exuded power. Kate gave as the reason for her own coming as: 'Plain curiosity.' She added with a serious glance towards me, 'I want to see what kind of woman Ian has found.' I knew what she was thinking.

She was remembering one long evening in June. I had returned from my ride later than usual, and she insinuated that there was a romantic reason for the delay. In defence I told her that Ian had a girlfriend. It was true. Peter had told me. I had listened for the sound of his returning car on the nights he went to Carmarthen. He was so organised. One night for our ride-outs and another for his courting. It did not matter to me yet I imagined this woman waiting for him as I waited for the sound of his returning car. 'Why didn't you tell me?' Kate had said and I replied, 'It wasn't important.' Kate had shrugged.

This woman, whoever she was, had not been invited to the party so Kate was going to be disappointed. I was glad that Kate had come however. She had kept from becoming involved with the family and maybe resented the fact that I was. We had one strong link with the past. To me the past was so innocuous. There were so few landmarks, no vital depths . . . until the end. That road accident which had crushed Richard out of my life. Then for a while, as a young widow, I had felt the love and protection family and friends could bring and Kate became important. She was a bigger part of her brother than even I had been. We comforted each other. We shared grief for a while, but her grief remained. It was dormant yet easily roused and she could remind me and rebuke.

*   *   *

In this farm kitchen Kate and the farm matriarch sat side by side. Sarah was heavy, her broad shoulders and strong, female hips supporting the mass of flesh that the years had entailed. Her eyes, narrow, white lidded, missed nothing. There was the spark of interest which showed always as they flicked from corner to corner of the room. Kate, alone of all present females, met her on her own terms. My sister-in-law had dressed with care that evening as if to play a certain part. A green dress, plain and clinging, emphasised her stylish figure, taking away the slight mannishness she showed sometimes; her face was clear-cut and different from any other woman present. Perhaps I was the only one who saw a light, a reflection from the room or disdain in her dark intelligent eyes. This glint dimmed when they met Sarah's as they conversed. There was mutual respect, both were speculative and I shivered a little as I considered their combined strength. I wondered where I stood in this family's hierarchy. I was always welcomed in the house. Even now, amongst all the sons and daughters, it was I who sat near the old lady. Possibly I posed no threat, but this was not comforting.

Sarah answered me when I said, 'I suppose Marie will be next.' She turned heavily to see what her granddaughter was doing. We both watched Marie, now tall and sturdy, as she tried to show some of the younger children how to sing a funny song with exaggerated actions. She sat on the three-legged milking stool, polished and rubbed until the grain justified its graduation from cowshed to kitchen. She waved her hands in time to the music and they were all laughing. On times like this I would give a lot to know the Welsh words. Sarah's tone was strong and complacent. 'It's easy to marry the girls,' she said. 'In farming we have to watch what the boys are up to.' She settled herself back on the oak chair . . . 'And I do.' I remembered then that Peter's fiancée was the only daughter of a man who farmed eighty acres in the next village.

*   *   *

51

When the cold, often wet weather came it deterred others but I found it exhilarating, especially when we were facing the sleeting rain and were buffeted by the hard wind which blew across Sylen. The wind resisted us so, sometimes I thought it resented us.

Other times when drizzle lay over the brow of the hill, 'Sylen weather', Ian would be somewhere ahead of me and I could not see him. The silence, like the mist, would be impenetrable. Celyn would give his high-sounding gelding neigh and there would be a muffled answering cry from Honey. On these occasions it was a case of one quick drink before our return. It was too cold for us and our horses to wait.

My trust in Ian increased. The years had passed and these days he often rode Celyn. He knew me well enough not to pull on the gelding's mouth and, if I was honest, I loved to watch my Celyn's action. Teilwng . . . the Worthy Holly. I was able to relax on Honey. Awkward as she was she knew me as well as I knew her and there was a genuine link between the two horses and their riders. The mare and gelding knew every inch of the road and stood like soldiers on duty as we drank whiskies warmed with almost boiling water from the tap behind the bar. The Welsh cobs were losing a little of their lively bearing, we all age. As we stood in the rough car park we chatted and sipped our beverage, they relaxed. Their jowls hung, trembling slightly; one hind foot lifted but the square forms of the Welsh cobs were solid as they slept.

'This must be the last time.' Ian said this as our horses trotted on the mountain path towards home, paces matching. I said, 'It's been a long time. Riding so much, speaking so little.' 'There doesn't seem to be the need.' Ian stroked Celyn's neck. He knew that was the way I stroked him and knew he did it to please me.

My hair escaped from the helmet and was wet. My riding hat had faded to grey-green over the years. I was glad I had the same motivation to ride. I owed so much to the uncomplicated equine companionship . . . of course I am, we were all part of a team. I said, 'It takes two riders, two horses to be safe.' He understood me now. Not so long ago, only a few years, he would not have followed my train of thought. He shrugged as he defined his answer. I meant one rider would watch the other and he knew this. Lonely riders would obtain all the physical joy but to have a relaxed contentment there had to be two people, two horses. Celyn and Honey so conscious of the other's strengths and failings with their particular empathy. The same road, the same inn . . . familiarity.

*　　*　　*

The red berries flamed amongst the thorns, sparse and vivid they brightened the hedgerow. The space between foliage emphasised the dying year. Shelter afforded by the tree trunks in the valley was warm after the stinging rain on the crest of Sylen.

I thought, like life, some stretches are hard.

*　　*　　*

A quick drink, rain sliding down the sides of a glass. When there was nothing to say now there was too much. Memories of other rides and other friends were evoked and instances we had not realised we had noticed were remembered. The children, who were not our children but part of our life, were discussed. They might have been our own.

I saw Ian's face become heavier over the years and his eyes which had shone like coal were less black. I felt myself more gentle, my vitality was certainly less aggressive. Part of ageing, I supposed.

We leant against the sides of Celyn and Honey and reminisced. I tried again. I waved my hand enveloping . . . 'All this . . . has meant everything.' and for the first time I mentioned, 'People must have thought . . . well, sometimes . . . even Kate . . . as long as we know.'

Ian nodded. I said I'd take the tray back. I collected the glasses and the empty crisp bags. Everything is just the same, I thought, just as innocent and is no more than mist in the breath of the mountain.

A Matter of Independence

All the outbuildings had doors with a secret. This one looked impregnable, solid oak weathered back to the colour of a tree trunk and one worn hollow where there should have been a handle. A finger inserted here would contact a slat which could be lifted off an inside bracket. The door then opened into the warm fecund atmosphere of the stable. Cobwebs plastered thick walls, swallows flew from side to side beneath the rafters, twittering, but not in fear and most often with an object in their beaks. The calves were separated, by age, into groups; two in the top partition; one in a side section where a calf which was younger and more vulnerable lay in a stall which was deeply lined with straw and, in the far end, there was quite a space, enough for six calves, some lying with that air of contentment that ruminating seems to achieve.

They looked up with a curiosity and one showed friendliness. It came forward, raising its head with an almost yearning expression. The smell was warm and animal, but not sour . . . milky. The walk-way around the edges of the pens was laid with straw, but this was fragmented into almost dust particles through frequent use. A pile of hay was fragrant in a corner. Rhys picked some of this and topped up the little racks. Round wire containers, which had been around the oil cylinders, too good to waste, made handy racks, just right for calves. At this stage Rhys paused and looked towards the shadows. It was as if he felt a presence which emanated approval.

It was an acknowledgement he needed. In spite of entering from the brilliance of midday in July and even though these were only slits, high in the walls, to allow in daylight, he needed no time for his eyes to adjust to the darkness inside the building. The second, necessary to close the door was sufficient. Now the shapes of the calves were evident, the Cheralin and the cross Hereford, the Jersey, calves which had slipped easily from their mothers, his good omen, been born during his normal working hours, or even those which needed the 'puller' which had been at hand, were rising from the straw and reaching towards him. Feeding in the mornings now was an extra chore, he turned once again towards the shadows and whispered,

'But I'll manage.'

Rhys listened to breathing sounds and rustlings. He remembered how many times during the last year, especially on cold days or when the wind came down from the hill or when rain was incessant, he had tried to forestall his father with the buckets of milk and scoops of nuts; he had not succeeded, the old man, only a little more white faced and thin in his late eighties than he had been in his sixties, when the frail appearance had belied his native strength, was there. David, the doyen, the cornerstone of the mountain family, would be bent over the mangers, his lined face intent on the animals he fed. Rhys tried to erase memories like these as soon as they were evoked. He was used to the rhythm of life, birth and death, but death was often synonymous with a gun or the slaughter house, not the slow fading of love. He tried to prevent his father being affected by the elements, from becoming cold, it was his wish to protect . . . to serve; it was the thwarted, outpouring of affection which had been a kind of sublimation, to supplant his love of a woman, children and assurance of his own line. His father was his unnatural destiny and now there could never be his own children. He had been resentful, almost rebelled, but contentment had returned. Rhys's mind was attuned to all practical demands and was not trained in analysis.

He worked now as if his father was beside him . . . the old man, the name given to him by most who knew him, as a mark of respect, had been a constant figure throughout the life of Rhys, representing security, but it was only since his mother's collapse and terminal illness that his father's absolute worth was realised and was missed.

For years there had been a perfect partnership, ever since his younger brother had eased himself out of the last quartet of the large family, four boys, three girls. They never remembered being children; vague recollections of crawling on the terracotta flags in the kitchen, bottom drawer of the oak chest into which they were placed for safety or as a punishment, had long since disintegrated. Then there were the three of them, sufficient to run the farm for so long and their home, the cream house with red paint round the windows would have been graded as a listed building, if anyone who knew about such things had ever seen it.

Rhys held the bucket for the calf. These old walls were his refuge, had been since he was a boy. Inside, no one could feel any weather, however rough, outside, not even the winds; no one could feel any tensions, there was only trust, the breath of animals . . . memories like little signposts. Mostly they were memories of peace.

Usually it was peace and satisfaction when the new calf lay in deep straw after the trauma of its birth; it would have been taken away from the mother before any bonding had occurred. Rhys would be just looking, winding down after the emotions and energy used during his administrations. Today there was a problem, the perfect Friesian was sucking from its mother when he entered the cowshed; this calf, having smelt its dam, suckled and been washed thoroughly by her rough tongue would feel the pain of separation. Its lusty bellowing would be answered by the mother for days before both would forget. This was one of the times when Nature would assert herself. He reached out his hand, not intending to touch, but to tilt the bucket; somehow the back of his hand brushed the skin, washed through to an immaculate sheen by the mother, and he could feel the silkiness. He felt that urgent need to communicate his joy . . . tell his father when he came out of the house to join him and then, the desolation, the knowing, all this elation had to be swallowed inside him.

*   *   *

He leant over the smoothed grain of the wooden barrier and remembered hearing the groans which came from the kitchen. The sight of his father, bent over the kitchen table as he sat in his corner of the settle; the blood which had spattered the blue surface. He remembered, sitting and watching, helpless, as Margaret, the neighbour did the little things which were all that could be done, a pillow to rest the head, the benison of cool water to sponge the forehead and wash the stains, attempts to retain dignity. Then there were the last words to himself (in Welsh), 'Bring the milk into the house,' his father's chore, his father's admission he had failed in this duty.

Then the emptiness, the relapse of his mother who could not live without David. This reminded Rhys of the ruthless dismissal of the girl he had intended to bring to Disgwylfa as his wife.

*   *   *

The sun in the late afternoon was a warm bath. It gave Rhys the sensation of well-being and his eyes shone. The pitchfork was an extension of his own muscular arms. The lower strata of bales, warm and crisp, were easy to arrange, the second demanded the services of the younger experienced men and then, only he and his brother were left; his brother's face showing the strain of the effort and in himself, the sheer exaltation in the certainty of his power.

There would be the swaying adventure of taking the load back to the barn; the change of drivers so that he could manoeuvre the *gambo* into the position for the off-loading on to the conveyor and the bales would be rolled off for the experts to stack them surely into the pattern and fabric of the harvest.

His thoughts concentrated on the moment afterwards with the hum of the tractor and piles of cut grass around him becoming plumper and plumper with the warm air lifting and separating. It was a good crop. Then, hovering, so that his eyes would notice her in time, was Eleri, a basket on one arm and her old thumb stick in the other. She was wearing the jeans and the blue check shirt he had seen so often. He drove the tractor nearer and shut off the engine.

Eleri, the untouchable, widow of old Silwyn, whose farm she struggled still to manage. Rhys had helped with Bryngwyn's harvest as long as he could remember. Between himself and Eleri there was, he would never had been able to put a word to it, the woman could, an awareness. In this delirious heat and intoxicating scent, the power of the farmer lifted him to the crest of his own world. On no other afternoon could this have been possible. He swung himself down from the tractor, ignoring the iron rung of a step, and came towards her.

No-one else was around; the drowsy heat kept the birds silent in the branches of large oaks, the last turning did not need more than one man and the rest of the mountain's farming fraternity was at tea.

Eleri must have guessed or felt the significance in their communication. She withdrew into the shadows under one of the trees. There were no words to mar his inevitable victory . . . submission.

The basket rested on a rounded hump of grass, Eleri, stolid and calm, proffered the cut sandwiches and plain fruitcake as Rhys moistened his dry throat with sweet tea. They remained, resting for a while, listening to distant tractors as other farmers and their families worked their own fields. Then, standing, smiling at Eleri, Rhys brushed his hands against his rough clothes, no longer thirsty, no longer hungry, yet with his own strange yearning for a life he could now visualise.

*   *   *

She had come into the cowshed once, just after they had two new calves. She had knelt in the straw, waiting to gain the young animals' confidence, laughing when at last the trusting faces came close to hers. He felt as if he owned the world that day, his animals close to her, touching her. She had eased her no-longer-young body out of the car and, as he drew back into the deep set doorway, it was natural for her to follow him. In the dark recesses the young calves came forward, curious to see the intruder. The floor was strawed down, the ancient walls meant silence and security, even the gap between the older calves and the young ones was dry and soft with freshly spread straw.

'I love a stable,' she said, 'These walls, so safe . . . and the sound of eating.'

'Yes . . .' he nodded, his eyes still watchful, then, pointing towards the interior, 'those are two of the calves I have just brought in from the Railway Waggon.' He made certain she saw the ones he meant.

'You look after your animals better now than ever.' She remembered earlier times when there had been too much indifference in his attitude towards animals. His face showed pleasure, and she added, 'Animals give you back something, don't they. What would you do without them?'

60

The two remained, close and in absolute communion, the calves shuffled in the straw and watched with bovine curiosity. How many years had they known each other. She thought, how few words they needed.

She sensed his need for reassurance and knew her 'love . . .' Yes . . . it was love, giving this reassurance to him. The thought, how innocent we both are. No one would believe this and suddenly she was aware of an immense responsibility.

At the same moment they thought of the pony in the other stall, the little mare. 'Only Geitha is out,' he said, and she answered, 'But she enjoys it there . . . but when the weather is bad . . .?'

'She's got her place,' he said. The stall he indicated was the stall he had lent her for her own pony, years ago when she had returned from a ride out or a hunt.

In the warmth of the stable on that frozen winter's morning there was an aura of love . . . it was a word which could be changed, more suitably for the biblical term 'charity', love between two strange and different people which was durable, which had surely been proved over a quarter of a century, emanating, spreading and penetrating the corners and in the couches of the stable, which was spent on the animals, the innocent calves; given back to the man and woman from animals dissipated or concentrated, they could not know. It was a love which could never be developed by either of their timid and shrivelled natures, only recognised and felt between those ancient walls in the fecund atmosphere. Both looked at each other, it was a long, half smiling, tender look which faded into the sadness of immense understanding. In this look they acknowledged defeat, as they reached out to touch the rough coat of the nearest, uncomplicated animal and, the gentleness of the caress hardened as fingers clenched in the tension to express an alien emotion.

*　　*　　*

But, even as a daughter of a local farmer, she had not found favour, not with his mother who reigned supreme in the cream farmhouse and had not one thought of abdication.

How could his mother and father who had shared their own unique dependence and companionship prevent such a devotion for himself. His frustration was expended in silence within these walls. Where was the girl he wondered, she should have been with him at this moment. Inside the house her breathing could take away the silence which seems a hollow coldness, a premonition of the grave. Who is to share his joy as he considers the black and white calf which lay on the straw in front of him?

Work might be a help. To think something physical which might drown those voices he seemed to hear in his mind. Voices which carried accusations against him, emphasised the things which were worries . . . like a conscience, nothing serious, just ordinary worries which might be more than a passing niggle of something not quite right. Voices no one else could hear or mind. Little things which were part of his life, like today as his herd meandered back to the field behind the house with his stalls cleaned and the wheelbarrow filled with all the waste . . . 'Waste'. The word echoed in his mind. Of course he is on his own, but it is usual. Nothing lightens the darkness of the day. Geitha, the little mare is in the stable, her couch next to the calves, he never rides her nor the class of mare which was once a source of exercise and pleasure.

There is no person in the world to talk to, all his work, his farming, his physical success is as nothing. There are half-formed thoughts in his mind, the unrealised dreams, silly words which other people discard and suddenly he knew they could be important if taken out of that context.

Not even Eleri could know one particle of his suffering.

*   *   *

And yet time passes. A farmer lives in the weather and by the weather. Rhys could not believe he would stand on the same spot on such a different day, when a breeze tempered early June heat, fanning his body with a caressing touch; he never thought on such a day he could experience the sensuous pleasure distilled from cut grass, warm earth, dry, even beneath the flat layers of winter dung; the clearing at the edge of the field which was the upper reach of the valley, a corral, newly created for the young calves who basked between a wide drinking trough and a central rack of last year's silage, now to be squandered. Most of all, he never imagined that he was indeed Rhys, the farmer could be master on his land or that he could see his own bales speared into their place. There was no one to see that smile nor see how the strained lines around his eyes and mouth had eased. He drew a fervent breath which was to thank God.

He felt gratitude for this moment in time which was significant. It is the emergence from that dark period. In this euphoria there is a future. His dream is of the perfect creature he will seek with help from friends. It is a time to learn all about artificial insemination and find the perfect pedigree strain. It is to be his show winner and the beginning of his stock, the line of perfect calves. In his mind the definite plan was forming. The plan formed had to be spoken aloud, words could make it happen. Then he knew he had his father's acquiescence.

*   *   *

Rhys moved over to the corner where the wallpaper was more yellow than anywhere else. No one had moved the clock to redecorate; no one had moved it since he could remember and it had not stopped until now . . . Rhys's fingers felt the fragile catch which held the panel over the interior and it opened. He saw the simple mechanism, the iron pendulum suspended by two chains. He pulled the leading chain, smoothed by the grasp of generations of his family . . . surely if ever help was needed, then the sound of the tick-tock. He listened now to the rasp of the winding chain, it was rough as it was rubbed; the silence was broken . . . tick . . . tick. Rhys vowed he would not fail again.

He returned to the corner of the settle which had been his father's seat. He sat back, the kitchen sounds were drowning the sounds of his voices and thoughts were sharpening dreams. He leant back, it was the end of the day and his work, he was the link with tomorrow. He considered the search for his flawless animal, dwelling on the problem at length in his own mind.

Autumn had merged into winter.

In the kitchen the clock ticked, he was the one now to wind it, taking the weight and pulling it as he had seen his father do, each night since he could remember. He would always want to miss his father.

The mornings when frost made plumes out of their breathing, the silent companionship which suited them both. The fulfilment when the milking parlour was washed and disinfected and the last round up of the day was a memory of scented hay, contentment and a sound of munching. When he did the round and lingered at each stall, he was certain he was not alone.

Night Life on a Welsh Hill

He watched remnants of the log being consumed in his grate, the shape of the log outlined by an edge of flame and he knew one touch from his poker would reduce the fire, which had given him warmth since his last frugal meal, into a pile of sparks. Twilight was early now and evenings were long; he chose logs, big enough and hard, so that once he settled against the brown velvet cushions on his chair nothing would disturb his quiet.

Now the log was a red cavity, burnt carbon to fall at any second. He drowsed for a while, pondering on his half-realised thoughts. He tapped out his pipe on a stone niche in his fireplace. He rose slowly and almost straightened.

Water in the kettle boiled quickly; he poured it over the tea bag in his mug and added a spoonful of ideal milk. A stranger coming into his kitchen would smell warm fumes from the log, tobacco, tweed impregnated with sweat and mixed with soil from his rain-soaked trousers which were drying over the door . . . and always, ideal milk. Through the undraped window he saw stars shine in the frosty night. Already a hard white crust threw back the moon's glow. He watched for a while a scene he had seen since a boy . . . and listened.

The listening was his life; the owl's cry in the bright night and a drawn-out, part howl or bark, a country sound, half threat and half comfort. From the thick walled stable he heard the sound of hay being munched . . . for a moment it stopped. He imagined the equine face lifting towards the window. His stallion, practically home-bred by himself, and his pride, winner of a hundred shows, the reason for almost all his high moments, the excitement, the feel of a silk rosette, the handshakes and applause, the passion and companionship which was sufficient and made him content in spite of his bachelor loneliness.

There was a rustle of silence in the old horse's shelter and that was the companionship he needed. He whistled his own signal, his goodnight, there was a soft whinney and the stallion's munching resumed.

For a while Idris stood in the doorway. The cold night sparkled into white shining distant tracks, brilliant moonlight compensating for any discomfort caused by the cold. His thoughts, continuous always in his waking hours, returned to other nights like this when, as a young man, he had walked from a local agricultural showground back to his stone cottage, leading the sire of Teilwng Celyn and carrying the day's trophy. His years were marked by memories in the ring. How well he had run with his partner; how prejudiced was the judge; how the winner on one occasion was unsound in his near fore and the judge was only looking at the name of the stud which everyone knew belonged to the judge's uncle.

But there was a night, he recalled, equally brilliant, when he had lingered late in the garden of the white house of a smallholding where a distant neighbour, Glenys, lived with her mother.

Families who belonged to the Welsh Cob breeding fraternity met on the days of the major Welsh shows and, in spite of heated arguments near the show ring, they subdued rivalries outside the arena. They offered shelter or grazing for animals who might have had to hack many miles from distant holdings; supper for the handlers, often young boys who were trusted by their parents to show the valued stock in prestigious rings. The ability to run with the stallion was not always possessed by older men. These were the times when boy met girl.

So the moon had thrown a searchlight that night over the orchard; the trees were silhouetted against a bright sky and spread their branches as if they were arms. To Idris then, super sensitive, aware of life, the power in all living things, the trees might have been breathing. The small world that was around him was magical.

They remained, his arm round her thin, strong shoulders and Glenys leaned against him, conscious of the power in nature; the air, the stars, the scent of grass, the sound of Teilwng cropping under the trees where the grass was lush; the warmth in their own bodies and the promise of young love. They remained until the last moment when Glenys had to go back to her house.

Now Idris's old face softened into a smile as he recalled that rare moment when he was a king and capable of conquering the world. How he had leapt on the back of his stallion and, as if having wings, Teilwng had flown over the hills to his homestead.

Even at this minute he could relive how he was on that day. His limbs, strong and pliant, legs capable of outrunning the wind, able to match, stride for stride, with his Teilwng as they competed; arms outstretched to hold the leading rein high; a body which could brace against all forces . . . the elation from success in the rings and the beginnings of love.

And another night which was equally brilliant, when he had lingered late in the garden of Glenys's home.

'Glenys . . . we could get married,' he said to the brown-haired girl as they stood with arms entwined, sheltered by the banked hedge.

She answered, 'Who would take my place here. Mother needs me now, the boys work hard, there's always food to make, washing and beds and, well . . . everything. Her voice was practical and resigned.

'But if we married . . . I'd take you away from all that.' He watched the grimace on her face, understanding her knowledge that the change from farmer's daughter to farmer's wife was a change, maybe in status . . . to be desired perhaps.

'If only . . .' she said, but in her circumstances not possible. 'There's no one except me. I wish I could, but I could never be so heartless,' and she added with clear conviction, 'I know they would make life hell, throwing my selfishness back at me for the rest of my life.'

'That's it . . . your life,' he had said.

For a while they stared at the valley patterned by moonlight. His eyes searching automatically for Teilwng.

His recall was vivid; he felt the shock of realising how he had failed in his responsibility, had not kept vigilance of Teilwng, who had been placed temporarily in the care of his friend and rival from the Kenwyn Stud. The words he would have spoken were forgotten, replaced by a premonition. He remembered Tom mentioning that morning that the Kenny mare was withdrawn because she was in season.

Afterwards there was the fury of Tom's father at the unlawful mating. There was the fury of his own family and now, Idris in his old age, laughed aloud at the memory . . . having to pay hush money; yet they had extracted the promise to have the right to buy the foal which was almost bound to be born in eleven months time. Teilwng Celyn, son of Teilwng, was born to become his own. He saved every penny earned during that year. He had worked long on their own fields and hired himself out like a slave to neighbours who, niggardly as they were, made him sweat for every penny.

Idris stared across the whitened fields, frost glaring now against the sky. He saw once more the brown-haired girl, too timid and too stubborn, and there was the ghost stallion who reared and cavorted and the mare with the loveliest conformation and the gentlest of natures . . . waiting. In his mind he saw the moment of their mating. And my life set in silver, he thought.

His thoughts drew him back to the animal stirring and scraping the straw in the stable. His voice had the softness of a lover as he said 'And you were worth it, my boy . . . every penny . . . every day of the waiting and even the sacrifice, for that's what it meant my lad. You were my own fulfilment.'

Oblivious until now of discomfort, beauty of frost and clear sky sufficient, he shivered, recalling the warmth of his kitchen. One final glance of utter appreciation and he returned to his lonely bed.

The Wheelbarrow

Ben should not have placed the last clod on top of his wheel-barrow. It was the one square of winter growth he had determined to wrest from the ground and which had finished him. Now its weight fastened his barrow like a lump of lead to the path. He told himself it was the recent rain which, soaking the earth, had made it hard to handle. It had been easier last year . . . easier than that in the previous year. He abandoned the barrow, turned his back and leant over the dividing wall between house and garden. Then, for a moment, it seemed as if he had moved away from sweat and silence.

He saw, through the kitchen window, Doris, his wife, she said, for forty-five years, but he could never remember. What did they want to bother at their age with anniversaries and such like. Her movements were quick as she went from the stove-side to the sink and to the cupboards behind the chairs. She would be baking, but not for him specially. He liked food when he was hungry, but it was Doris who revelled in mealtimes. Laying the table, best cups on Sundays, proud as a peacock when their son came with the grandchildren, or the vicar or any other visitor. She did not cook because she had to. She cooked because she wanted to . . . as she did everything else. He watched her go to the door, lift her hand towards the hook from which he knew the dog's lead trailed. He heard Mick's bark and he knew Doris would soon be outside in the lane, walking the dog. There was no need. There was no traffic. The dog could go by itself.

Spring was here all right, but cold this year. Everything had its season. Doris had planted her bulbs in the autumn and they had come up, yellow and straight. Birds flew around the bird-table where she had put out scraps. He grumbled to himself, women did not know what work was. For them life was nothing but twittering around, stirring the soil and ambling in lanes. They had the best of things.

Damn the sun and the earth and all things growing! Women had nothing to drain them of energy. Things they did were easy. Like Doris, able to enjoy herself. When she had nothing to do except to look busy . . . busy . . . busy . . . all day long.

He tried with a surreptitious movement to shift the barrow . . . no luck. He wondered whether to remove some of the contents, but even the thought of that top clod was too much. No wonder his old mate Tom had had enough four days ago. He had read of it in the *Western Mail* during his avid perusal of the 'Personal Column'. Joe Barnes phoned and told him that Tom had been setting the garden in time for Easter. But it had been cold on that day. Tom should have known.

His thoughts went ahead. He expected, he hoped, fervently that the funeral would be a good one.

*   *   *

He waited near the window so that he could see the bright shape of Joe's grey Austin as soon as it rounded the bend at the junction. He would hear a change of gears on the hill outside the lane and, seconds later, a change of tune in the engine as the car came under the arch of trees . . . old trees, thick growing from banks of ground-elder and dog-weed. Nothing wrong with his hearing today. His ears were tuned into noises, like Mick's were when the postman came through the gate. He had shaved and changed and he was able to wear his dark suit without the overcoat. Except for funerals, he had little chance to wear that suit, and it was still as good as new. At funerals it was the uniform, essential most times. He wondered who else would be coming today. Usually Joe had a full car by the time they reached the church.

Outside the church the men were gathering. Tom had been well liked. Most of them had worked in No. 2 Slant at the old colliery in the past and, later, when they were older, ended their working days on the surface . . . relics. With all the collieries closing it was only now the younger men understood what that meant.

Ben laughed with the others as they brought out their old tales, stories which involved Tom mostly. It was Tom's day after all.

'Remember when he came out early to go to a funeral . . . John's I think it was. He got on the bus and sat next to the Manager's wife.'

'Fair play, she even paid his fare. But never said a word.'

'She was a good sort. She'd ring over and tell the Bath Super-intendent if her husband was coming on his *tramps*.'

'He wasn't bad either – for a manager. He treated the day-wage men as well as he could.'

'Who'd have thought he'd have gone before us?'

'Boys . . . the queue is getting shorter.'

'Aye.'

For a while the faces tightened. It seemed as if they saddened, but there was an anticipatory gleam in Ben's eye. The moment of quiet passed and they filed into the Church. Several of the choir members, friends of Tom's, were there. The singing would be up to standard. He hoped they had chosen good hymns. As a group they found their places and Ben's spirit soared, rising with the music and the male voices.

They filed out afterwards in twos or threes. Each man was anxious to prolong the moment. They mentioned Tom's past glory when the rugby team was formed. They remembered his humour and strength. Ben told them how the two of them had concreted the path to the Lower Chapel.

'Three afternoons and I don't know how many barrows. Lazy man's journeys most of them. It was holiday time and a scorcher of a summer.'

'There's thickness too in that path.' Heads were nodding around him in approval. Other feats were remembered and assessed, jokes aired. Latest bulletins on contemporaries were exchanged and it was time to leave. The group, animated in dark cloth, circled and streamed to their cars. Ben and Joe saluted their mates.

'A good time to show . . . we stood by him to the end.

*   *   *

The car wound through the lane. Young green leaves filtering the afternoon light made things seem misty. 'Oak before Ash, we'll just have a splash. Ash before Oak, we're in for a soak. We need rain now. Things dry up in no time.' Joe was thinking about his garden. 'I've put in the potatoes,' he said. His companion did not answer.

They were outside Ben's house. In the front, his wife's efforts with the flower beds looked promising. She was digging away with her trowel. She was singing a song, the one she always sang while she weeded.

Ben felt as if he had left his world of comradeship and laughter. His shoulders felt heavy and his legs were stiff as he rocked and climbed out of the car. From the gate he could see the pale brown earth in hard untidy mounds. He saw the wheelbarrow, solid as a rock on the path . . . just where he had left it.

Boxing Day

All was cold sunlight. The dark conifers and church tower thrust through the white mist which cast a spider's shroud over the scene. The cobbled square exuded excitement, a sharp holiday excitement, more potent because it was December and the ground under one's feet was frosted and crisp.

It was a scene from an opera; the characters, wrapped in bright Christmas clothes, came on to the street in ones or twos. Their faces were shiny after a day of indulgence; they were relaxed and ready to absorb a new experience. There were men in tweed hats; farmers in corduroys; dowagers in thick stockings and teenagers in coloured thick stockings; most women in sheepskin coats or lined anoraks and men in roomy sweaters and sheepskin coats. There was one slight man in a raincoat who was holding the hand of a small girl; he seemed to be protecting her as he was ensuring she would miss nothing.

Glyn Morgan was on the outside. Huddled against the tingling air, he ignored the glances of those who belonged, though he could not miss the way their eyes flicked over him; glances which acknowledged the curiosity of 'that other world' as one of those things.

Curiosity! Glyn would have said they were right. Why else would a miner from the slag tipped village of Bryndu walk two miles from his stacked-high anthracite grate to mingle with strangers on a cobbled stone square on Boxing Day.

Curiosity . . . and a walk for the child. It was right to give her a chance to see something a bit different. All the way across the fields he had answered her questions and smiled at her mystification. He knew it was something she had to see for herself. It was right she should have something . . . to remember.

The cobbled square with its nebulous mist over the street, which was now full. The air of expectancy was piquant as the set prepared for the arrival of the leading characters and a hush as though each player held his breath, ready for the first rousing chorus.

The chorus was the murmur as the first rider clopped into view. The crowd made way for the horse and rider to take their stand. A polished chestnut coat flared against the grey street; the steam spread from the animal's warmth to be lost in the morning mist. They were alone for a while, horse and rider, still, save for an occasional scrape of a hoof. The rider cursed himself for his over punctual arrival. He had mistimed the distance from the inn where he had left the horse-box. He wished he had taken the second whisky.

Glyn's eyes screwed with sardonic amusement. The fellow wasn't feeling as cocky as he looked, perched on his precious bit of bloodstock. The miner settled back with the crowd to enjoy the entertainment.

Another horseman, this time on a roan Arab which resented its public appearance. It danced and was overlight on its forehand, it reared enough to interest the watching group, who did not appreciate the fact that their safety was in the none-too-competent hands of the skittish mare's rider. Glyn moved to a more strategic position. He kept his grandchild close to his side. The miner recognised danger, it was as familiar as an old friend. His lined face, aged by long hours underground, lifted. He knew from experience with his pit pony, back in the thirties, that this was an animal ready to turn her rounded backside any moment to endanger those near with her flailing hooves. She rose her head and stamped, a gesture of defiance which Glyn liked. For a second the separate worlds touched. 'Kick your heels my beauty. Don't let them break your spirit.' He was not worried, he was safely positioned. The toughened group of 'this is my world, horses are in my blood, ruddy-faced and straw-haired women' could look after themselves.

The sound of coins being shaken in a wooden box was heard as a slim girl in jodhpurs passed it through the spectators. 'Support the Hunt' fund or something similar. Glyn tensed himself as the box came nearer. Normally he gave readily to every flag-seller outside the Pay Office on Fridays or to the Salvation Army girl who braved the pub on Saturday nights. His pockets were littered with raffle tickets sold by every football club in the district. His granddaughter smiled and held out her hand for the coin. This was their special game, when Glyn allowed her to drop the money in the box.

'Grandpa . . .' she said.

Glyn's eyes, however, were fixed on the horses and she pulled at his sleeve, lifting her head to look into his eyes. 'Grandpa . . .' but the girl with the collecting box had moved further along the square. The clenched hand which had been thrust, stubbornly, in the depths of Glyn's pocket, relaxed. These people must pay for their own pleasures or fights.

The chatter was louder.

'Is Mike coming?'

'I saw his horse-box outside "The Farriers" as I passed.'

'Where's Robert taking them, I wonder?'

'Marvellous day . . . wish I'd taken a mount myself.'

'We'll cut up to the Graig after. See them in full cry.'

'Ah . . . here's Bobbie.'

There was a louder murmur from the crowd as the Master and Huntsman arrived . . . and the pack. Glyn said nothing as the voices sang around his ears. He was the stranger and this was another life. The illusion, made real in the colliery by Union talk, miners with motor cars and pit head baths which sluiced the dust off men before reaching the streets was disintegrating inside him. He was back in the feudal world of colliery owners and landed gentry. He shrank, as though to keep them protected and sharply distant from his person.

But Dhew . . . there was a smell with those hounds! He studied the pack. They did not look like the fit little brutes on Christmas calendars. They were a scruffy lot . . . young too, some of them; they sat on their haunches, for all the world like a lot of lap dogs. One of them was restless, slipping amongst the crowd. It drew close to them. Glyn's grandchild stretched out a hesitant hand. Her brown, bright eyes turned towards her grandfather, asking his approval; he nodded and she stroked the square head. The hound snuffed gently and moved on. The whistle of the huntsman called him back.

'Grandpa. Why have they got red coats on?' The child found her voice in the distilled magic of the morning.

'That's the proper get-up,' said Glyn.

'Where's the fox with the tail?' asked the child.

'Under cover . . . hiding, out in the country. They'll look for him when they go.'

'Grandpa . . . why do they wait?'

'Part of the game,' said Glyn.

It was about a quarter to eleven and thirty or forty horsemen made up the field, filling the square. The spectators lined the pavements more thickly. The mounted men and women, confident in their numbers, were talking with animation to each other. Some of the men were in their hunting pink and others in tailored black. The women looked immaculate although that word was a little incongruous so soon after Christmas Day. Some, evidently farmers with a taste for the sport, were mounted on sturdier animals with longer coats although even these were groomed to look as fine as possible, but there was a strength about these men and their cob type horses. 'Why should they look so different?' thought Glyn. How could a man's face, two eyes, a nose and a couple of ears show whether he was belonging to one set or not. It was not always the texture of skin or the elegance of some of the ladies . . . a look at those horny harridans over there will prove that, cheeks like leather!

And there was the warm, steamy aura of horse dung.

His granddaughter stared at the solid strength of the leader, well mounted on a top weight golden dun.

'Why has he got that big whip?' asked the child.

'To show he's the master,' Glyn answered but kept wondering.

A few of the hounds lifted their heads and bayed, 'like blasted wolves,' thought Glyn.

Then a small horn was lifted to the lips of a man on a golden horse. The hounds gathered themselves almost as soon as his arm moved and the riders drew their reins more firmly. The horses collected and one or two bucked in anticipation. Glyn felt a quickening inside him, in spite of himself; in spite of his unrealised envy; in spite of the fact that this was representative of a past which had bitter associations; in spite of the alienation of his dark world from this reckless, extravagant rush though wet, green, winter fields. He tightened his lips . . . in spite of danger being so strange it could be taken as a pleasure. He held his granddaughter's hand in a harder grip.

There was the sound of the horn, the tingling as the Master moved forward, sweeping his riding hat with a gesture, theatrical, ceremonious . . . 'but fitting,' thought Glyn.

The design of the pageant formed and moved. The crowd filled in behind it but Glyn remained still. He would not acknowledge the stirring which urged him to move with the others. His grandchild pulled his arm and he held back.

The colour which had crashed through this grey-white December day was streaming past the churchyard, the Red Lion, and through the backcloth mist. There was the clopping sound over cobbles.

On the square Glyn was alone. His eyes belied the stubborn pride which kept him still. Then he surrendered. He hurried forward and now he was pulling his grandchild's hand.

'Come on,' he said, his voice ringing with a new sound. 'Come on, we'll go as far as the bridge.'

The view from the bridge, as Glyn knew, looked over the riverbank and to the track leading to the Graig.

Once he had reached out he was reluctant to let the moment pass. His senses were unfilled. He craved the last spectacle as the men and animals spread out across the fields, the rich tapestry broken by green.

Besides . . . it was right the child should see . . . to remember.

The Last Season

'When?'

Gwyn looked at the poached top soil where the cows waited with bovine patience each day before they came into the milking shed. His wife Ruth was speaking, repeating, as was her habit, the general theme over and over . . . words. Even without her saying, he had understood what she meant at the beginning. She had to have her say.

His wife dropped her pails on to the cobbled yard. 'So you were listening when I told you.'

The evening sun reflected in the small pools which lay between the cobbles and dung. In this half-light, their yard could look beautiful. Nights were drawing in. Last evening it was dark by eight o'clock. Summer was ending. Everything was ending.

'Not long.' Her voice was sharp with excitement. The group of cows was spreading widely as they ambled across the field in front of them.

Gwyn said, 'They're looking well. Been a good year: grass high as your knees. Barn's full. No sickness with any of them . . . fine calves.'

Ruth continued: 'The Council says it will be ready as soon as we are. A nice little flat with cupboards inside, even for the coal: electric light, a cooker and washing machine . . . everything. It has a fridge as well. Shops around the corner . . .'

He picked on the word which tore at his stomach – Council! His voice contained the contempt that a man who wrung a living from the earth and elemental forces for sixty years would feel for a body of men in suits who seemed to have nothing to do but shift through papers. He tapped his nose with a gnarled forefinger. 'Busy-bodies!'

Now his hand fondled the head of Patsy, their old bitch who had been his staunch companion since the day she crawled from a disused manger in the milking shed where her mother had whelped. Ruth's voice was softer as she said 'You'll have to do something, Gwyn. Even though she is your life. They'll not allow pets. Nothing like that.' She wanted reassurance 'You know, don't you?'

'I don't know anything.' He kept his face averted and she guessed how his blue eyes would be blazing hate against the fact that the land he had farmed was to be offered for sale. This bitch, who had loved him with pure passion, was to be sacrificed. His wife followed the direction of his eyes and tilted her head in an attempt to gaze directly at him.

'You should have done it then . . . when she went blind.'

'How could I? You might forget but I'll not. How she stayed with me when that happened. I can still feel the rocking and the shaking and the power of that tractor when it went wild.' As he spoke about it, he could sense his skin prickling and his forehead moistening with a cold sweat. 'All day she waited, guarding me when I lay knocked out of my senses and lying on the ground. If it wasn't for her whining and barking, you would never have found me. Now . . . I'm her two eyes.'

Ruth's expression set in her tight-lipped manner. She regarded the yellow walls of Bryngwynnen, the farmhouse which must have been at one time, more than a farmhouse. '*Another* winter; your chest; my rheumatism. It's time Gwyn . . .' Inconsequentially, she added, '. . . and those damned servants' bells in the kitchen . . . as if there would ever be anybody to answer them!'

Gwyn replied, 'I can't think of the house without us. 'Twas never his, though he was the landlord.' The landlord had been fair enough all these years, however, letting them have the place for such a low rent, and now it was right that he should want to sell when prices were high and there was such hunger for land.

'One winter . . . no, one or two autumn gales and things will crumble. I thought it was us who needed the place, but Ruth Bryngwynnen without us . . .' His voice tailed off and in a husky whisper he added, 'It won't be long.' He walked towards the pile of logs heaped against part of the arched entrance to the stable, 'These took me six days.' She said, 'We can take some of them with us.'

Patsy pulled at his sleeve. 'Alright, girl, I'm coming.' He knew she wanted her evening walk to the group of stunted oak trees and brambles which grew around the old mine shaft, long since disused. Once he had needed her company. On evenings when things went wrong; when the hayrick burned; when disease affected his herd and the Vet had spent that terrible day . . . that day of destruction at the farm, that was his lowest hour. The night he had taken his gun with him as he walked to the spot. When he had waited hours as the frost whitened the twigs and leaves, for the courage which would finish the struggle forever. It was the warmth of Patsy's tongue on his hand, her body against his and the whimper which had made him remember life.

His hand twined fiercely through the fur of her coat. 'Stay with me always, my blind one. I'll not let you go.' His voice was almost a croon.

'That's what I mean, Gwyn.' Ruth would never make him understand. 'Our time is finished here . . . hers, yours, mine.' She stretched out her hand, yet before she touched him the party they were expecting from the estate agents arrived. Ruth drew a long breath and squared her shoulders. She could be stubborn. He would not change but circumstances decreed that they must go and she would never do anything to prevent this.

As if he had not heard, her husband continued to speak. 'The house; everything which grows; the stones which stand and make the wall of those old buildings; the logs, cut from the branches of the elm which fell in the last storm . . . all here because of me. The house is big, I do know. But Ruth, all these years I never noticed. It gave us room and when I came in from the land it enclosed me.'

'It has been hard to work,' Ruth added. 'If not for yourself, think of me.'

The car was turning just outside their main gate. It was a big car, wide and blue. The mud splashed against the shining body-work.

Gwyn thought of his wife as she had been. Life, strength, energy. In the summer when they came in from the fields they felt the evening sun as it flooded through the wide windows on to the hall and staircase; in spring, they looked out at wild daffodils which coloured the hedgerows and the January snow-drops by the river bank. In winter, they built up the kitchen fire with logs and were warm or they shivered when they left the fire to do their chores.

'I can't see this couple putting overcoats on when they have to go into the pantry when there is an east wind.' Gwyn's face was set.

When the couple came out of the car they looked with avid eyes at the classic lines of the farmhouse. The sun was by now quite low in the sky and from the windowpanes the glow was reflected with brilliance.

'I thought we would come before you settled down for the night.' The woman had a London accent. Before Ruth had a chance to warn her, her flimsy shoes were sinking in the dung. Gwyn tried to merge into the shadow of the gateway but the man saw him and came over. He was a young man with a dash of aggression about him. He must have done well to be in a position to bid for this property at his age. He took out a packet of cigarettes and offered one to Gwyn. The farmer shook his head. The young man was conscious of the hostility in the blue eyes but he persisted.

'Is there a history?'

What is history, thought Gwyn. He shrugged his reply.

The man regarded the building with its magnificent proportions. 'It should have. Not that I go in for too much of that kind of thing, but . . . his waved vaguely, 'Just enough to lend atmosphere.'

Gwyn's head turned towards the coppice around the disused mine. He did not know that he shivered and that the stranger was looking at him with quick expectancy. The farmer was recalling a cold clearness of a winter's night and saw sharply, in memory, the feathery edge of frost on fallen leaves and the bright round moon through a frame of blackened branches. That night he had seen nothing but his own despair. Gwyn answered the question, 'I don't know. When we took the house over sixty years ago, twelve families had come and gone. Some couldn't work it. We did. We stayed.'

'The house has got something. It's old. Large enough. Actually, I'm impressed. We'd get a grant of course. Do it up. Modernise things a bit. More power points, etc. Clear up that pile of wood over there. Soon no-one would know the place.'

'No. I suppose.

'No suicides, ghosts, murders? Anything our friends would relish?'

'No.'

Gwyn remembered a night, or was he visualising a night. A night as long as day, not yet spun by time. The moonlight and dark shadows of the trees from Lower Cwm. He could see the man in front of him looking from the window of the main room. An older version, more poised, even more full of confidence, of the man before him who stared out across his land . . . land that was his because he had bought and paid for it with cash.

'If it won't be you, 'twill be one like you,' he told the visitor strangely. 'Someone with money but no-one with more love than I had.' It was the young man's time to shiver.

'They say . . .' Gwyn's voice was low and grating, '. . . on a winter's night a man can be seen walking towards that clump of trees over there . . . over there where the old mine shaft is.' Gwyn pointed out and the listener followed his hand with eyes that were frightened as well as eager. 'A man walking slowly, leading his dog . . . and there is a sound of two shots . . .'

Logan Rock

The field was full of cows. No one minded them, they were the buttercup and daisy cows, brown and white with soft beige faces and with udders full of fairy milk. One could imagine elves pulling at the long, clean teats on midsummer evenings.

Evenings when the sky spangled with starlight and the Plough, a clear saucepan, pointed over the Atlantic towards Wales. I could imagine, in spite of all this bright light, times when the black cloaked covens returned from night raids on the fields of Wales where they could bloat themselves with milk from Taffy's cows; instead of gulls' wings would be the whirr of broomsticks.

There was a concentrated accumulation of ancient activity in this small cove. But now it was afternoon and hot with summer. The Atlantic was like opal and laced with a spreading foam. Nearer inland we could see the sand under the water and long shelves of rocks.

If the scene was portrayed on paper by an artist nobody would believe the colours. Green luscious grass, yellow flowers, white flowers, pea-green sea and rocks sparkling; patterns of foam over the shallows and, to the east of the bay, the threatening, rearing Logan Rock

The car-park linked us with this present tourist century. The attendant with his bag and tickets and guidebook commentary found all the world his stage and, finding an extra player that afternoon fastened, ancient-mariner like, on my husband. With his sunglasses and camera, Ian tended to make the most of incidental characters and details to mould his own stories; I saw he meant to enjoy this conversation.

As I was the born-and-bred Cornish partner in our marriage, I guessed the car park gentleman had placed Ian in the 'up-the-country' white hat and easy tan brigade, and would patronise my husband with an oily charm. Still, we could explore without him, my mother, sister Cara and myself.

We were not out just to go beaching but to enjoy a drive and a picnic. There was a small Methodist Chapel near and we decided to enter.

It was one of those chapels which showed that people still cared. The pews were oak and had once been pieces of ship's timber. This was a part of Cornwall where smuggling was a way of life. The black-robed witches might even have raised the storms. The chapel made the link between past and present; the ships boards on the floor were scrubbed and white, and protected by plain coconut matting. This also was right, simple and plain, as was the table altar, covered by a baize cloth and, apart from the visitors' book, supported nothing but a vase of fragrant, cottage-garden pinks.

The visitors' book open at the current page. We all inscribed in it, Cara, Mother and myself. We looked back idly at the names on other pages. The chapel was solid and square and had a queer life of its own; it was not difficult to hear the old hymns ringing out across the cliffs on a winter's night nor to imagine the oil lamps shining through the dark.

Ian came to the door and waited for us to join him.

'Not too many cars,' I said.

'That's what the old chap was saying. Considering the weather is so absolutely perfect. But, as he said, it's not the sort of place for the usual holiday tripper.'

'No, I suppose not,' said Mother. 'It's a long walk right over there.' She looked towards Logan Rock with the cliff castle towering behind it.

'But that's what we came for. We must see it.'

'I don't need to see bits of Cornwall here or there.' Mother was searching for the warmest corner in the rocks. 'I just have to feel them.'

I knew what she meant; we felt the same way about this place.

'It's a long way. Do you really want to try it?' Cara was kneeling beside her bag and searching for her apples and a book. 'I'll stay with Mother.'

I wanted to be able to tell everyone I had been and mentioned the way down to the beach looked difficult.

'It is,' said Ian. 'The car park chappie told me' He was focusing his binoculars on the rock and when an elderly man, who seemed to be into some kind of professional research, passed, he said, 'Just look at that camera.'

We women looked around us. Cara nudged me, 'That's more in our line.' A couple were climbing down to the in-shore rocks. They might have been on honeymoon. The boy was solicitous; she was a gipsy-type in her long maxi-skirt and silly flip-flop sandals.

'Hardly the right climbing gear, even for small rocks.'

'Who cares when there's a helping hand.'

Cara had definitely settled herself by Mother and Ian was ready to begin. I waited, watching with female envy a mysterious woman on her own, who now came towards us. She carried painting materials and walked slowly as if absorbing every minute of this glorious afternoon. She seemed interested in the chapel too. She asked us about it, questions about Wesley and the Methodists. Home counties . . . to judge from her voice. She was wearing dark clothes with some of those folksy copper bracelets.

Mother was more interested in another couple we saw, a boy and a girl who looked German. We all agreed on this, though no one knew quite why. I said, 'It's the arrogance in his walk.' Mother said, 'It's those shorts. I can see him dancing to their German bands in their beer gardens.'

Ian was studying the girl, 'It's her.' She was blonde and Nordic, wearing one of those embroidered blouses, traditional garments adapted by modern women with the same enthusiasm as their mothers or grandmothers before them.

Hot and drowsy but utterly content in our speculative study of the few people visiting, we sorted ourselves among rocks which might have been carved for our purpose. Seats in stone with quartz-flecked slabs inlaid, the cliffs glittered with the chips of crystal when they reflected the sun.

Ian and I went to climb up to the Logan.

In the shadows of the rock the sun made little difference. It was cold and eerie; so easy to imagine the stormy nights and shrill screams above the sound of the waves and the rattle of broomsticks and rustles of old women taking off over the spray into the wind. But there was a more sinister mystery here, a scent of fire and sacrifice and ominous hollows which had held frightening secrets.

When Ian was out of sight I bared my behind and touched the rock in the manner of real witches. Not that I believed in anything like this but that was the kind of place it was.

Ian took some photographs and we returned. The afternoon passed quickly. We drank tea, took more photographs and spoke a lot about the very distant past and witchcraft. There were many legends about this place which were easy to understand; it was a mixture of beauty and evil. There would be the old people singing their Sankey hymns so lustily, their feet on ships' timbers torn from wrecks . . . if not by themselves, then with their knowledge. There was the green-yellow edge of sea and the drowning chorus from mermaids, the lost pool and, above all, the rearing, black toppling shape of Logan. Now there were even fewer people around and the sun was lowering. It was time to return.

The car park was almost empty when we passed the chapel. Ian said, 'I ought to see this before we go,' and I accompanied him into the building.

Some of the strength in the place seemed to have drained away since early afternoon. The place was shadowy and the pinks in the vase were drooping. Ian insisted on signing the book. I opened it for him.

We both stared at the page which Mother, Cara and I had begun with our own names. There were foul drawings and crude remarks scrawled right across it. There were blots and curses and a couple of swastikas and the beginning of an obscene verse based on the Lord's Prayer.

When we came outside neither of us spoke. Mother said, 'Wasn't it lovely in there?' Her smile faded when she saw our faces. Ian shook his head.

I scanned the cliffs and the headland. I saw the people we had seen. In the dimmed light against the western sky the figures were larger than life, darkened, evil and inscrutable.

It was as if a crazy artist had blotched the afternoon on grey paper. Each figure was grotesque. The cows loomed above us on a sinister green horizon.

In Spite of Everything

Alan liked the soft glow on the pavement when autumn lights were reflected and more than liked the emptiness. No 'gawpers' now to impede his morning dawdle and, although the wind was beginning to bite a bit, there was the clear view of the Atlantic from the end of the street, which compensated. In shop windows the things which were seen were left-overs, pieces of no consequence. Locals treated flimsy cotton fashions, useless hats, porcelain ashtrays with pictures of pixies and mugs from the local pottery with contempt. Tawdry souvenirs were for gormless folk. Tourists were right in the season and could be tolerated. Traders in this locality realised it would be futile to think of attracting their neighbours with an even adjusted-to-weather display. And this lack of aggression also suited Alan.

He turned towards the sea and breathed more deeply. He detected the smell of salt and the tang of seaweed which was stronger than the faint reek of last night's tobacco fumes. The street in this seaside town was now clean without exotic smells filtering through kitchen ventilators and realistic without sun-tanned goddesses with strange accents to strut alongside or lean against a companion Adonis. Alan felt authentic, true to himself now that there was no longer the summer tensions of extra traffic and crowded cafés. Time was condensed when hours of daylight were lessened. He revelled in his space and ability to walk without half-naked bodies jostling him. It was good to exchange gossip with fellow natives now that they had time and a respite from pandering to those 'up-the-countries'. Time was unleashed and Alan was in tune with the freedom. For many years after his retirement he was bound by the clock. He experimented with his own rhythms . . . in the morning when the door opened into the snug, thick-walled building where polished bar tables awaited the elbows of the first customers, and in evenings when the crowd in the smoke-filled tavern cheered as he made his way to the piano stool. On his piano top he knew there would be an array of glasses of spumy beer.

For emptiness read clarity and clarity was truth even though truth sometimes rendered an inhibition which slowed the flow of music to his hands.

He was now in his usual pace and the music which sprang from his fingers could be the downbeat for a blues singer. Though he smiled for the benefit of friends who expected him to enhance their recreation he could not shake off his misty harbour mood. He played 'Summer Time' and those listening almost heard the words behind Gershwin's music; or saw a white film over water when he played 'Mist On The River', his fingers lingered over 'The Londonderry Air'.

Conversation lapsed all around him, recommenced . . . but there was no 'buzz' no 'zing' and little laughter. Harry, landlord and friend, looked across and met his eyes and Harry's face might just as well have shouted, 'Lighten up, Alan.' The pianist knew his music was spreading depression around the room and well . . . so what!

The woman who crossed the floor looked round and comfortable, her late holiday hinted at retirement . . . the season for the young had finished. 'Mr Pearson?' She was addressing him. Mr Pearson . . . that did it . . . he was back in the classroom ten, twenty, thirty years ago and, like the repeating taste of onion or garlic, he remembered enthusiasm. She burbled on, 'Oh, I did hope to see you here. I guess that's why I came out to visit . . . well I always did think it was a godforsaken seaside dump . . .'

Loyalty for his own bricks and sand and sea flooded through his body . . . forgotten pride, just in time, 'You have to live here,' he said.

She waved a podgy hand, 'Oh, I know, I know.' Her face, browned from the last of the holiday sun, beamed. She turned to her female companion, gold pince-nez on peeling nose . . . 'Our Mr Pearson . . . the Pied Piper, the magic schoolteacher, our children and their children still talk about him.'

'I've retired.'

'So I've heard, and today's generation of kids will never know what they've missed.'

Behind his chest, vessels of heart and lungs seemed to unite to form a barrier, warding off the impact of her words. It was as though he rejected any credit. He had accepted the aura of failure, adapted it to suit his night club and dim lights, blues music and drooping image, the village character, slightly colourful, dispensing bucolic stories and late night rippling on the piano against a rising convivial sound in the public bar.

Her words held their own and the barrier receded. His fingers were lighter and a melodic tune trilled briefly as he considered. It was the children. He remembered the woman's own son and daughter, their bright laughter at one of his poaching tales and herself, one generation before, round-eyed as she led the Christmas percussion band with her triangle. There had been that thread of excitement. The kids now had returned something. He raised his eyes and considered her face . . . searching. It was trusting, sincere, bland and confident. A faint memory shifted into focus; he saw the square, red-haired companion of some of her out-of-class episodes. 'You married Timmy Retallick.'

'You remembered,' she said.

* * *

94

A change of light showed through the windows of the bar. Not yet dusk but a dropping of intensity and the leaves on the old rambling rose outside were darker. He was in place. His own place. Just now his shoulders were hunched forward, his hands clasped and relaxed as they rested on his knees; he stared in front of him, he might have been looking at the music, but his eyes might just as well have been closed.

*　　*　　*

The piano top had a gloss, lucent to accentuate the gleam on ivory notes and the sharp glint on black notes.

He had his routine and each evening he left the house at nine o'clock after he had helped his mother to clear the supper table and wash their simple collection of 'pots' . . . he liked that term 'pots' . . . unsophisticated, rustic, somehow pertaining to the world of the woodland retreat and the language of the peasant. He liked the word. It was not affectation. He thought of his grandfather and wished he had told the woman he had met that it was his grandfather who had earned her epitaph. Already it was an epitaph which his dear ex-pupil had conveyed to the relaxed audience in the saloon. His grandfather, with the cocky head which tilted sideways like an alert squirrel, who had drawn him from his square little world with wise, ancient Pan-coloured promises of green magic. He knew his own feckleness had made it easy.

With this gnome-like man he had placed his dubbed boots on grassy glades when the white moon lit the pattern of tree-tops, when the owl called and flew in her silent circle. The old man had whispered instructions, filled his pockets with his 'boy's own' tools of the trade. As an apprentice he had held the lamp and clutched small Patch whose stumpy tail had beat time to the music of the elfin night. He had shared the sugar sweet tea from the tin billycan and listened, over and over again to traditional words, and the lessons learned on those brilliant nights had

95

surpassed the academic wisdom of inky classrooms. Was it the attraction of the alien which had been his inspiration, or was his brain unable to take the classroom routine which was subsequently wasted? Only the hands had learnt to pull music from the air and fingers to translate a poacher's fantasy to lure the up-the-country tourists into a village pub.

His grandfather was the genie of the leafy glen, who sang inside his head as his fingers struck the evocative notes which drew the passing strangers into the yellow warmth of the tavern.

He sat and played, free of his undemanding responsibilities, unleashed from the demanding work and not rewarded. And now . . .

'Mr Pearson. You . . . not behind your desk in school. The children in the years to come will never know what they've missed by not being taught by yourself. You had magic . . . the flair!' The words repeated in his mind.

It was not himself, it was not his dear bright, bird-eyed grandfather who wooed the spirit of the night. His laziness was the catalyst, 'Go to the sloth . . . thou sluggard.'

His fingers were tributaries and music flowed from a mystic lake in his brain. That's what they said. Harry, his friend, almost his partner, though not in any business sense. Harry had followed his star, so he said on one serious exchange of confidences. There was the usual dream, every young reprobates' dream, to own a pub, to escape from his particular prison. Harry regretted his action at times and said his prison had been soft and lined with carpet; there had been wholesome food . . . no porridge. His jailer had been the hazel-eyed girl he had married when he was eighteen and too young.

Harry had told him that, sometimes, on a hot summer night when the swathing hordes of holiday people pulsed through the stone passages and pounded with impatience on his bar counter, his mind harked back to a regular city life when he thought he had not been his own man. Alan knew Harry so well, he recognised that wistful look, truculent eyes which became softer above his curling rebel's beard.

As though they had a life of their own, Alan's fingers played old London tunes. Harry's medley, friends called it; customers joined in, raucous over their beer stains. 'My Old Man's a Dustman' . . . 'A Nightingale Sang in Berkeley Square' and the pièce de résistance, 'The Lambeth Walk'. He would forget that Harry took him for granted; how love for that man was a reason for sitting behind the piano and becoming a non-person, a tavern pianola who churned out music to fill the ears with sounds his customers wanted. 'Yesterday', that always gets them going, especially at the end of the night . . . 'I Did it My Way . . .' this one affected him always, it was his special and, in spite of the cheerful comments, the constant plying him with the mellow brew, the genuine appreciation, he recalled how once he sat behind a desk on a small dais and filled growing minds with all the snips and snippets he thought important.

His fingers then wove a pattern of sound which led away from the last medley; they picked up the simple tunes he had played in the schoolroom. As he huddled over the keys he felt a stiffening of pride which re-enforced his body. He had studied and worked for this music. He also had been of substance . . . once. It was not a case of 'Go to the ant, the sluggard' as family and friends might have it, they called it betrayal . . . he called it his essential decision which was never decisive.

Those words spoken by the rose-brown country woman returned to his mind, they sounded unshakeable . . . she had made him a success. He knew she was right. In his own way he had given something to the generations of bright faces. He tried to recall details, fragments of experience, his own peculiar quality; these were the things he must have passed on, but there was only the philosophy of a tip-tilted, squirrel of a man who boiled water in his billycan and made tea which steamed in the forest and had filled a grandson's mind with his own generation's thoughts.

His grandfather's dreams were true and Alan had used his classroom to perpetuate them. They said he was inadequate, suggested early retirement which he was glad to take. His bright-eyed grandfather, young in his years, would have laughed and slapped him on the shoulder; his widowed mother had sighed when he had cleared his desk. He tried then to remember what he had taught; he could not remember. All he knew were happy thoughts and there were tunes in his head which echoed the chorus of living things in their small patches of woodland . . . and the tunes had fixed pictures in children's minds. He remembered good things and that, when he left, some of the children cried.

His fingers picked up a few bars of a midsummer folk tune, his broad, half-peasant, half-pixie face creased in response to a green sylvan memory. A half term holiday in the middle of June when the nights were full of light and shadows and the leaves on the trees might have been made of tin. Nocturnal creatures rustling in the undergrowth and the owls hooting with indignation as he conducted his current class of seven-year-olds through the woodland paths as he recreated one of his own juvenile adventures. The music, encouraged by his rising delight strengthened into 'The New Mown Hay'.

Unwittingly, smiles appeared on the faces of the regulars; they all recognised his sorties into their past childhood. Even the visitors stopped talking as they listened. For one moment a scent of damp moss and earth superseded the pall of cigarette smoke, the blue spirals dissolved into a white and peaty mist. He blessed the gift of music at that moment which, most times, he took for granted. He blessed the woman whose kindly words had led to this brief evocation.

Tonight he had heard his epithet. The eyes of the shiny faced ex-villager could never lie and she spoke for generations.

His body felt strong, the keys on the piano struck some new chords, and there was a note of triumph in the song.

The Chained Fields

He smiled. Sylvia looked at him and wished he would do that more often. His face was far too serious.

'What?' The light faded and once more his lips were firm and sad.

'It's too beautiful.'

'How can something be too beautiful. Besides . . .' Her eyes looked over the flat expanse around them, the chained fields, a stretch of country which led to the rough tin-mining area which had long since been deserted. There were the Leats of course, a canal of sorts in the usual state of torpid inactivity.

'This was busy once.' She looked at the dark, glassy reflection, wondered why such mucky water could light up in answer to the sun and the blue sky. The duck weed had not been cleared for ages. 'Further on, there's a tree trunk. We used to walk over it . . . dare each other. Do you understand?'

His head turned towards her. She thought his eyes were deep like the canal itself.

Why did she say that? The sun shone through the fabric of his shirt. The skin underneath, warmed, slid against the material; he felt the inside of his wrist as it lingered over the velvet corduroy of his jeans; each touch intense and sensual. The day was perfect. She was perfect . . . in her class. He was not patronising. An earthy presence; strong body and brown limbs; movements so active and light, the surprisingly sudden gestures; nothing like a Dresden Shepherdess but living tissue carved by a god preju- diced towards the soil and all growing things. Her hair was heavy and thick and shone as if the sun had brushed it. He wanted to twine his fingers through the separate strands so that he could feel the warmth. But she would misunderstand. The fledgling female in her would draw more from him than he was prepared to give.

She was watching him, her eyes curious and he guessed she needed to goad him.

'The water is not exactly pristine.'

'You're like a cat.'

He turned his slate-grey eyes towards her, frowning and knowing exactly what she meant.

'A cat?'

'Feline . . . super sensitive . . . paws raised.' She arched her wrist and fingers in a mock gesture, 'hating to have wet feet.'

He laughed, a sound which finished with abruptness into silence. But she came over to him and linked her arm into his.

'I shall dare you.'

'Won't make any difference. I do not indulge in kid's stuff. Good heavens child, who'd want to get wet on a day like this?' He looked towards the canal and shuddered.

'Don't mind me. We were children when we crossed over. It was fun. You know . . . seemed terrifying. I don't want to get wet either.'

He supposed she did not, but hoped she would cross the flaming thing and fall in. As long as she didn't expect him to pull her out.

'We will do it.' She ignored the exasperation in his sigh. Perhaps it might move him a little. All the time he was silent and beautiful, wanting all her attention and never really seeing her. Now, for example, he set his face towards the canal. Without a word or change of expression he separated himself. She became more childish and spiteful. What had she said that was so drastic.

'It's all right. I won't insist.'

'Doesn't matter.' His eyes drifted towards the skyline, rough and uncultivated.

'Why do you like it that much?'

He turned back towards her, 'It's so exactly right. You know, absolutely rural . . . no noise, no cold, no heat . . . a sort of growing. Life like a pendant hanging over these fields. And the canal, silent now, secretive.'

'You see all that?' His words echoed inside her and the echo subdued the guilt which stopped her expressing thoughts which might have seemed sentimental or theatrical and prevented any attitude which might be considered posing . . . showing off. Anything which might emphasise that feeling of being an outsider . . . even in her own home. She remembered hearing her father's laugh as he recounted the story of looking over towards the flat desolation of field and moorland on one of those nights lit by a neon brightness of the moon; the grotesque tree shapes making shadows like Celtic wooden statues. In the distance the shimmering lights of the town formed a tinsel edge to the mist and there was a magical silence over the land. Lights from farm cottages had seemed peaceful, all sound was absorbed in the wrapping dusk. How the broad flat land was at once mysterious and personal, open to the wide imaginations of the world. The story of this incident had sparked her imagination. She herself understood, but her father's voice was scathing as he described all this and his voice was cruel as he mimicked the words of his companion, her sentimental old uncle 'It's so utterly lovely . . . I could almost cry.' 'Cry . . . the silly idiot!' Her eager appreciation receded and she had even joined in the mocking laughter.

It was real and it was moving with the sun warm like today and being able to smell the heat trapped in the grasses and sense the lovely soft wind take the hair away from one's cheek. If he could realise she was not as insensitive as he made her feel.

'I like it too.' Her voice challenged. She did like it. It was a wide place where she could run, no one to criticise, and there had been plenty of activity here once. One could sense it somehow.

The canal was protected by a wide section of bogland on either side. Reeds and rare ferns and marsh marigolds grew in profusion. There were kingfishers and other birds which darted around the surface as if they knew that here they were safe.

They walked on. 'Sinbad' she called him because he had travelled over so many countries and was learning about life the hard way, not from books as he had explained, began to sing. It was a tuneless, wordless kind of jingle, but it suited the rhythm of their movement. He wondered why he stayed so long in this town, this country market town with dead canals running until they were lost in thickening branches. It might be because here life was still quiet enough to be heard; music of the earth and growing. He supposed this was it. It was refreshing and there was a rest from his eternal need to prove something. Adventure in strange places was a threadbare experience. So much strong colour drained by hot suns and only afterwards was there any romance. Still, there was more to be done. Lawrence of Arabia had needed a lifetime of desert before he found anything . . . if he ever found anything. The need to move away from all this, too mild and cleansing. Good to be with a girl, if only she was not so blatantly female.

Sylvia matched her steps to his. He knew she wanted to be kissed. It seemed so difficult to establish just the right relationship with girls.

From the moment he had walked into the library where she worked she knew she wanted him desperately.

He was so thin and fine . . . sensitive, almost like a woman. His hands, as he tentatively pulled down a book from a shelf or returned it, were delicate and perhaps sensual. Sensual was a word she had seen written but never heard and she had never used.

To break the memory of the room full of books and dusty with academic thought she broke into a run. Away from him over the path trodden down by generations, she ran . . . caught in the fabric of moving. Then she waited. He came towards her, looking pleased.

'I'm impressed.'

'By my speed?'

He laughed and flung an arm around her, 'No, by your beauty.' His arm moved away and the spontaneous gesture ended. His compliment might have been addressed to an animal.

'Why didn't you run?'

'Too old.' He smiled at her again, reassuringly, as if he had expected her to be offended.

She said without sharpness, 'I please myself.'

'Of course.'

They were close now to the place where the tree trunk crossed the canal. She said, 'It's gone smaller.' It had. 'It's almost safe enough for you to try.' It was quite safe. The reason for the battle between them seemed to have disappeared. After all the years the canal was smaller and the tree trunk was wide and solid. If this was to be a challenge it was to be a small one. She went towards the edge of the bank, light and dancing almost, she walked over to the other side. Turning was more difficult, the branches were thin and one snapped, but she managed to re-cross. She stood beside him, laughing, though her eyes were anxious.

'Where does that place you?' His voice was cold, the lines around his mouth hard.

Obviously it had not placed her anywhere. She had walked over the black, oozing depths and returned. That was all. It was difficult to know what to say, his attitude made it seem so childish. He appeared to be so hard when she knew he was gentle.

Some workmen were walking from the other direction. Their voices were loud in the early summer atmosphere, but they were joking between themselves and came across the two of them so suddenly that their mood was not broken. Their brown faces were cheerful as they looked at the young couple. Sylvia smiled back. If she had seen them once she had seen them a hundred times . . . at carnival time; in the market; mending roads or cutting back the growth in the hedges. One of them, sizing up Phil . . . Sinbad, with the infinite cunning of those who learn everything from nature, recognised a quality which set the boy apart. He took off his tweed cap and with a regal gesture bowed low before the boy, expecting at least a smile. Phil's face was drained and set. The grey of his eyes darkened to match the waters of the canal.

'Stupid oafs,' he said as the men tramped on, 'the British working man is absolutely without charm. They mock everything they cannot understand – which is everything.' He thought one at a time perhaps, once in a lifetime, one of them, separate from the herd might try to reach out across class and age . . . one might try. They were so pleased with themselves and content in their masculinity.

There was nothing she could say. Sylvia had seen the knowing smile on the workman's face when Phil's annoyance was obvious and she remembered her father's reaction. She also was uneasy. If he would kiss her. Other boys were too eager. It was nice to feel safe and all that, but there were limits. No, it was not nice to be safe. Not when one's energy was concentrated like the rays of a sun in a glass bottle and there was this fierce need to give; not when the boy was so indifferent, so utterly self-reliant.

His eyes were closed as he lay back, the tension in his face smoothed by the warmth and scent of the day. She could look at him and he would not see the anguish in her expression. The mound against which they sat, sloped like the back of an armchair. The grass here on the rise was bone dry and they could watch the dark shine of the canal. She was restless and pulled the slides out of her hair. Lifting her hands she let them run through the thick warm strands and then with a bored sigh she lay back against the bank, staring at the sky and shading her eyes from the sun.

She was aware of each sound; sudden splashing noises from the water caused by insect or fish; a blackbird darting through thicket with a brief burst of chatter . . . his breathing. And he was supposed to be experienced. Women could weave rings round boys always. But this was making her sad, this longing to be touched. She wished she could do something; to lean against him perhaps. She thought of how he would withdraw. She reached out her hand and shook slightly at his shoulder.

'I wanted you to walk over our bridge,' she had to tie him to a definite failure. 'I did. It was easy. I'll do it again . . . to show you. The canal can be crossed easily.'

He looked at her. One of his hands moved out and a finger traced her lips. She was looking at him now, not expecting a caress, but wondering what he would do.

'You should have been a boy,' he said. There was a strange yearning in his voice.

The afternoon became quiet, flat, as the people round here said when the sun recedes somewhere but no one knows quite where.

Two thin figures trudged along the canal bank back towards the town. They looked so much alike.

The Visit

It remains a source of mystery. What made me decide on a wild November day to visit Sibyl Moore, a colleague of mine who had retired many years earlier? It is true, she is a person who will linger in one's memory long after one has seen her, but on this particular day? I could not get her out of my mind. I kept thinking of her, wondering what had happened to her, even wondering if she was still alive.

For days small things reminded me, inconsequential things, like her neighbour's child who stamped his foot in a tantrum and smiled like an angel as she passed. Her smile which could have been the smile of a young woman when coquetry tempered the wisdom and guile. I remembered her stories, the incidents which revealed an eventful life, tragedy which she recounted so that it was almost funny, so that those who listened laughed. She was an enchantress.

I set out early that afternoon and, after a monotonous bus ride, I found myself crossing the stream which led to the mountain-track which led past her home. All day I was fighting my impulsion to make this journey. I thought of all the things I could have been doing and of the time wasted in sitting in the bus, driving through colourless streets on a grey day; I remembered how unpredictable she was. I might get a wonderful welcome, but I could just as easily be sent packing, told to return to the way I had come.

Because of the lateness of the year, black clouds were scudding across the grey sky, and the deepening light was filled with a miserable whine of the north wind. I felt cold as I made my way up to the isolated stone building on the slope.

I followed the tumbling mountain stream and entered the rickety wooden gate, the path with uneven flags which led to the door. I tread carefully, as if I might delay the actual moment before I stood outside the door. Rooks in the surrounding tall trees cawed mournfully and echoed the heightening disquietude which was possessing me. What strange exhortation had led me to take this autumnal journey.

Against the low wall of the house a large garden broom or beson leant, the pile of leaves it had gathered together were drifting back into the garden, leaves whirling capriciously, having nothing to do with order or regulation. I noted the garden was well tended and herbs of all descriptions were dying back into a winter sleep. There were no flowers, not anywhere.

A large black cat sat on the doorstep and gazed unblinkingly at me as I knocked on the door, the tap was timid and made little noise.

A voice cracking and high-pitched, called from within, 'Who's there?'

I steeled myself and had to continue, 'It's me, Margot Trewhella, I used to work with you once, don't you remember?' The door opened, inch by inch and the well remembered sharp-featured face, with large grey eyes, peered out; the same hair, tipped with the yellow streak of nicotine; the same bright, bird-like expression. I had a queer feeling that she would shrill 'Be off with you.' I was poised for flight.

I need not have hesitated, her arms were wide stretched and welcoming and the smile was warm and friendly. 'Come to the fire girl, and warm your bones. It's good to see you.'

She led me into a room which was almost too hot, a glowing fire burned with fierceness in the grate, the draught from the wind caused the flames to leap dangerously high. There was an old Welsh settle near the fire on one side and I was placed on the oaken seat. Opposite me was a comfortable rocking chair. The floor and table were bare, but scrubbed quite clean. A cauldron of soup or something which smelt strong and appetising, was suspended by means of a strange contraption over the hissing flames.

Within this magic circle it was easy to relax. The little hostess darted here and there and finally a pot of steaming tea was brewed and a plate of her homemade bread and butter was brought to the table. Sibyl was talking nineteen to the dozen. 'Why haven't you been to see me before, girl?' I made the long journey with two changes of bus stops as my excuse.

'I knew you would come today. This morning I thought of you over and over again. And now you are here.'

'Well, that's funny.' I told her of my own compulsion, the unaccountable force which had brought me here. As I was talking, her eyes were unwavering as they fixed on my face. I became embarrassed. I thought she did not believe me and I was defensive, 'It's perfectly true, you know.'

She laughed, the sound was high-pitched and engaging. 'I believe you. Look, I'll show you something.' With her typical quick movement she went from the room and returned with a pile of mint cakes. 'Pitch in.'

The cakes were delicious and I wasted no time as I chose one after another. She seemed to enjoy watching me. She began talking, almost as if she had to make the most of her opportunity now that she had an audience. I remarked, curious about her way of living, so lonely and so contented, 'I suppose you don't see many visitors nowadays, it must be lonely up here?' My voice contained a touch of condescension, the wondering pity which a person whose life is packed with mundane incidents, all of them involved with a home, children, shopping, a life which is absolutely secure, might feel for someone who must have nothing. My own eyes shifted away from a bright scornful glance, but when she answered her tone was assured, 'My dear . . . even if it were not for the young people and old who call at all hours of the day, I could never be lonely. They want advice which I can give because somehow I see things clearly and I make my medicines from herbs which grow around, and if they are not near my back door I know where I can find them in the woods. They have faith in me . . . I have faith in myself. My mother and grandmother were the same. Those I help with their ailments or their worries say I make them better.' She dismissed my implied criticism as if I had never spoken. She rose quickly, birdlike . . .

She lit the candles, for the afternoon light was fading. We chatted and laughed. I was under the old spell of her personality. She reminded me of some old shared experiences we had had, and brought me up-to-date with many bits of gossip. How she knew so much surprised me. After all, I was the one who lived amongst people.

Time passed quickly and because I did not relish a nocturnal journey down that mountain path, I made the first tentative move towards ending the visit. I was fascinated but I forced myself to stand and collect my outdoor things.

I bade her goodbye, closing my mind to the disappointment in her wizened little face.

I paused at the hallstand and put on my woollen cap, and in the small mirror I noticed on my face some of the laughter had lingered. I thought nothing strange about the black cloak and tall pointed hat which had hung beside mine.

109

New People in an Old World

Outside it rained and there was a wind. Along the harbour only a few feet of walls showed above oily waters and, away from the shadow lights from clubs and cafés, sent their green, red or yellow streaks towards the open sea. The horizon, crossed by smoke haze and dusky cloud patterns was a glowing furnace, more industrial than a normal seascape and reminded her of a working hinterland behind all the colour.

Night sounds began. At first a thin symphony from distant traffic, increasing to a crescendo before fading to make the background for slamming doors and shouts and laughter and conversation. Sounds which the water made clearer. Soon the music of jazz bands started, wailing and strumming, noisy and evocative; and there were the cooking smells, a dockside haute-cuisine, a combination of peasant and exotic food from pans in the surrounding kitchens. A night atmosphere was established . . . colour, food and music.

For young people in an old world . . . or was it the opposite.

Madeline picked up her mug of coffee and, with an apologetic shrug for any intrusion into privacy, roamed around the room. She saw theatre programmes strewn on chairs or tables; booklets from the Edinburgh Festival: travel brochures, too glossy to be untidy, were evidence of quality of life. The sprawling settees spread with flagrant sumptuousness in front of long windows and a balcony which overhung the narrow street which was the wharf.

She thought she should have been in a more personal environment. This was like a trip in a time machine. She had thought

110

of a quiet hotel in the Lake District or even Bournemouth . . . and with all this hankering for the past, 'why didn't I go to Falmouth?'

She touched the furthest outer wall which was roughcast and almost had never changed. This felt solid, not wet with salt damp though she thought it might have been. She liked this wall and in an impulsive movement she placed a palm flat against its abrasive surface. In spite of numerous coats of decorative material the smell of seaweed, sacking, malt and any other dockyard odours seemed to linger.

The opposite wall supported shelves which were crammed with books, long illustrated art books, flat paper information sheets, Penguins, hard-covered books covering a multitude of subjects and proved wide acquaintance with different cultures. She envied her niece for this. Pictures on the walls, a brass relief in a prominent position. Music-Centre (top of the range of course) and good looking souvenirs. Everywhere was untidy in a nice way; a spate of other people's cultures drawn together and Madeline wondered . . . just who does housework in this flamboyant flat? She knew Gillian's husband travelled to sell their *Sound* as they called the specialised speakers which had become desirable in the up-market corner of the music world. Gillian herself accompanied him most of the time and contributed a lot with her intelligent enthusiasm.

When Madeline first walked on the balcony away from the sophisticated interior of the flat, from warmth to an autumnal evening, she breathed sensuously. A rainy wind from the southwest caught the open window and banged it against an iron support. She held it steady. Though the wind emphasised smells of salt and fish, the air was so clean. She inhaled with relish and almost tasted it and as she turned she felt raindrops cold on her shoulders.

The feel of rain was familiar but, arriving from a grey mining village which was her own drab and quiet background, everything, even with a heavy drizzle, was colourful and foreign. In the half light, just enough darkness to see shuddering reflections of lights, from ships and the quayside; just enough light to see the masts of ships bounce, and even in the harbour's shelter, all was exciting and exotic. It made her recall her young years. She could relate.

A harbour and what had been docklands full of the sounds of working men.

*   *   *

Gillian had taken her cup and refilled it. Silences were easy with her niece. The older woman sighed, there was a touch of longing. It had been traumatic, seeing old warehouses so changed and the catalyst for nostalgia.

'This is so like our own harbour town. When I first looked out from the balcony, everything came back into my mind. Can you imagine this warehouse when it was a warehouse. All the buying and selling. Imagine sacks of flour piled up, over-running with rats at night.'

'Ugh!' Gillian said. Madeline saw that her rambling remark had evoked a response. She smiled and considered the girl's reply, 'It's bad enough now when they load their stuff in the morning . . . waking us all up.'

'But the smells are still here, malty smells with the whiff of sea and fish of course.'

'And probably beer,' Gillian laughed. 'They must have loaded wagons full of barrels to send all over the county.'

She was too flippant. Madeline was forced to defend, 'But I've seen it. Men working, shouting warnings to others, cranes swinging, iron grapples clinging, bales from ships to the warehouses or landing areas. Oh, you don't know what a lovely sound is the ring of hammers. Il Trovatore and all that.'

'So long ago,' Gillian said, and thought it might have been in the Middle Ages. Her aunt repeated, 'It makes me remember . . .' and she continued, 'not so long, or it doesn't seem so.' She mustn't sound as if she were tedious. 'It was like this . . . years ago when I was young, I thought it was more innocent . . . of course it was . . .' She looked out over the maze of masts between the harbour walls and the outlying bar of the sea. The thought was incongruous. How could her niece understand a world which was hungry and frightening and wet, when the smells of cooking came from a bakehouse or a fish and chip shop and any music came from a rattle of a piano in the bar of a slimy walled pub on the corner of the quay. 'And there was,' she paused as if wondering whether to continue, 'well there was a girl . . .' Once again she stopped. To explain the impression made by the girl who seemed like a princess to her when she had come out of the doorway was difficult. A picture imprinted on her mind. 'The girl,' she tried to express, had been dressed in a red coat with a fur collar which she had pulled around her small neck and face with such a ridiculously sensuous gesture. Her hair was caught on each side with combs, her cheeks were painted and her lips were red, though her teeth were brown and a bit uneven . . .' Her voice tailed off at the last memory, at the time she didn't think the smile had spoiled her. To the young Madeline she was everything that was glamorous. She remembered the sailor who came over and threw his arms around the girl's shoulders and she still saw, in her mind, the way the girl leant back against him. There was a little passion in the knowing smile on her face. It was a cameo. A photograph burnt into memory. How could Gillian ever understand?

'Yes, tell me . . .' Gillian looked over towards her aunt. She thought she was beginning to sound interesting and that the weekend might be less boring than it had threatened to be.

So many years had passed since they had last met. All that time her aunt had lived in another world, a dull, isolated world, dreary, in a rainy country corner near the mining village. She herself had travelled in so many different countries. Each year they had spent apart might have been ten. Yet here was an affinity. She liked her aunt.

After a pause, Madeline asked, 'Do you remember my aunt . . . your father's aunt? Really remember. I know you brought her flowers on Mother's Day, small gifts. Your mother insisted on all that. Aunt Bridget loved it.

'Yes, I do remember, slightly.' The younger woman thought of all those dreary afternoons in the old lady's kitchen. The smell of the dog.

Madeline turned away from the window and looked directly at her niece. She drew a breath and contemplated how much time had passed since then . . . years. Far too long. 'Did you listen to all those stories. They were real stories. So many people coming and going then. Funny people sometimes.' Gillian's expression became remote. If the girl did not remember those stories she wouldn't remember anything. Who could have forgotten Vi Bently . . . with her man's tweed coat and a hand tailored skirt, who smoked and smoked and was always borrowing money off Bridget or the sea captain who spent many weekends at home and wanted to marry her aunt. Old man Jenkins. She thought of him these days with a compassion not shown at the time. She tried to tell Gillian.

'If I could picture them I would be interested. It seems so far away. I can't remember myself as a child . . .' Lynne is into theatricals, she might be interested . . . costumes and sets and all that.'

'But this wasn't theatre. This was real . . . so real.'

She remembered how she had loved Gillian when she was smaller. But even then the world was different from the old. It was swimming and surfing and walks over the cliff. Not diving off the quay and listening to old people tell stories. 'Lynne would like to hear, I promise you.' Gillian's voice was dismissive. Madeline knew she was a bore. Was there any way of returning.

Perhaps tonight they might create a new memory; they could make plans for tomorrow. She wanted to make a contact and at the station she thought it possible.

Herself waiting by the buffet, watching the changing patterns of people, so many groups at one time with so much to do. She had thought how each individual was propelled by a purpose and then . . . two figures hurrying, young figures with that air of 'looking' about them and they headed towards her. The dark-haired girl ducked her head with that remembered peering movement and an expressive hand rose in a small gesture. Years since that last meeting were erased. Madeline and Lynne and Gillian became a tight group. Then, for a while, they relaxed and studied each other.

'You remind me of me,' Madeline and Gillian chuckled easily. So the years had not wiped out a closeness of humour and style which was seen, also in a similarity of looks.

'And Lynne,' Gillian indicated her daughter, 'Lynne, at last you meet your aunt. My favourite aunt.

So many years. 'It's been ages. Lynne was being carried in your arms when I last saw you.' Gillian took her case and there was a deference to Madeline's frailty. A reversal of roles.

*   *   *

A tide-slapping morning; bumping sounds of small craft loading the plastic containers of fuel and baskets of food, crates of squash or lager and all the gear necessary for a day out at sea.

Sleep had been difficult. Her mind was sharpened by the different scene and she had been cold in her bedroom. The open window allowed the sting of night air into her room and she was loathe to close it. She dressed and waited for signs of movement in the flat. She needed to go outside and breathe in the whole of the white tipped, salty scene.

*   *   *

They shopped and when they returned with the food Lynne was already in the flat. A young girl eating a thick slice of toasted bread, wholemeal of course, with her coffee. Gillian went into the kitchen immediately and her daughter's voice, pitched high with animation, filled the kitchen as she recounted every incident that had happened since she left them on the previous evening. She had seen her father. Gillian had divorced her husband a year ago. It was obvious she wanted to know everything Lynne could tell her about the meeting.

Lynne obliged . . . a mother listening with indulgence to her daughter, yet it was more than that. Madeline heard about Gillian's marital problems during the last evening. All Gillian would say was 'He just hasn't grown up.'

Here in the kitchen she saw Gillian was content to listen to her daughter, perhaps with keen attention. Mother and daughter were animated as Madeline watched them through the dividing hatch. Gillian was busy making coffee. Sometimes she looked towards her and smiled, shrugging a bit helplessly. Lynne was on a high. They discussed each other's outfits and might have been two sisters.

Gillian had flair, her clothes had an expensive simplicity which was continental. She could be a French woman or walk in · a street in New York or in any of the world's capitals. As for Lynne, in spite of wearing an assortment of garments, displaying a clash of styles and colours could never look anything other than one of the privileged.

Choosing a good place to lunch was a major problem. Madeline was hungry. The opulence of the flat provided good background comfort but food seemed unimportant. Even the weekend shopping was confined to purchases of red peppers, muesli and maybe vegetarian sausages. Madeline thought of her own normal trolley loaded in the supermarket with essentials for her own pantry. She would have burnt far more calories in any case by this time of the morning. She anticipated the lunch . . . good company and good food. She moved towards the others. 'You both look so thin,' she said. They did, dieting and vegetarianism was fashionable and the prospect of a good steak was out and yet, when lunch was discussed, the meal they wanted was something piled high and hot in a steaming café. Madeline approved.

*   *   *

Over lunch conversation was easy, the fresh bread and the wine and the delicious fish pie must have been created by a treasure of a chef. The vegetarian diet was flexible. Lynne said, 'Have you read the book written by the miner's wife about the strike? Fantastic. The way they stuck together.'

'Lynne's the professional marcher. She's for the underdog.'

Her mother looked towards her daughter, there was a lot of pride in her expression. 'All I do is a bit of electioneering . . . handing out of leaflets, mostly making coffee.'

'I know about the way they stick together.' Madeline was possessive about her own world. She knew all about life in a mining village during a strike. She had worked with miners and knew them as they faced hardiness and tragedy in their dark environment. 'I think the strike was marvellous!' Lynne tucked into the piled up plate of a real Fisherman's Pie cooked in a place where there was always a glut of fish. 'They hated it.' Madeline's voice was fierce. 'Not one of them wanted to strike. It was to prove their loyalty.' Gillian explained to her daughter, Madeline knew many neighbours and friends who worked in collieries, 'Did you know them?' Lynne looked across the table as if noticing Madeline for the first time. Her aunt said, 'Yes, I knew them well. They knew me. They gave me a party when I retired. It seemed as if the whole village was there. I was . . . well, quite proud.'

'How brilliant . . . how romantic.' Lynne surprised them. Madeline thought, *no, not brilliant, not romantic*. Maybe she had fantasised in her own way about the docklands when I was young, but the memories stayed. She realised she had a new role, for a while she revelled in the importance of being a story teller. She was someone whose past had a relevance. 'Did Gillian tell you about my aunt in Falmouth?' She began to build on the hesitant references made earlier to her niece. She recounted incidents . . . like stories, her own legends, her life, personal impressions stimulated by the eager attention of Lynne. 'Your mother should have told you this so that you could be telling your children. It's up to you, you know . . . to pass the stories on.'

It was as if she heard Aunt Bridget's own voice in her head as she spoke in that over-crowded Cornish kitchen and the flames at the side of the oven spitting as the old iron kettle boiled into the grate. 'I was told these things . . . until now I never knew how much I would remember. Nor how much they meant. It's another world.' Lynne repeated this. Her brown eyes were fixed on Madeline's and the older woman thought it's just as if I am telling her a fairy story. Nothing is real in her life.

*   *   *

It was evening and they were walking through old buildings in the one-time shabby part of Plymouth, which was the Barbican. Sometimes a stone bowl, standing outside a house and filled with geraniums, showed how the middle-classes were taking over, even in this remembered rough quarter. Gillian was enthusiastic about Jazz. 'Real Negro and Harlem . . . poor musicians that no one ever thought anything about and the moderns taking over as they have. Oh . . . and the saxophone . . . oo . . . oooh. It's loud and exciting and the way they pick up a phrase,

118

take over . . . work it through in their own way. Against the establishment and classical . . .'

Madeline's voice was enigmatic when she said, 'With me it was seaweed and malt in a dusty warehouse. With Lynne, she has her own interpretation of the lives of miners and coal dust. Race relations will be next. I wondered if anything would chip into your middle-class veneer. I'm glad something has . . . even if it's only Jazz because it is fashionable. Negro music and the streets of Harlem.' Gillian laughed without much humour.

'I meant to say it's a good night out. You'll see when you meet my friends. It's a good club. Mmmm . . . how it gets through to you.' She echoed her daughter's words, 'It's another world for us. Echoes of New Orleans.'

Blue dark crept through the street and corners and by-ways were more shadowed. People moved toward night venues. Once again the sound of men and women were taking over from the day-time traffic. The two women were drawing closer together. They neared the corner where they would turn down towards the quay. A man and woman came into view. He had his arm around the woman and she was leaning back against him. They were roughing each other up a little. The woman wore a red coat with a fur collar turned up to meet the curls in a tight permanent wave. *Déjà vu 1*. They were weaving their own path towards them.

Madeline's attention was fixed on the red coat with the fur collar and the way the woman was cuddling into it. That picture merged with the smell of salt in the background and a dream picture in her mind. She did not notice that Gillian was embarrassed. Not until the woman pointed towards them and almost screamed, 'Gillian, my love. Where have you been?' Then the couple swayed closer and a smell of gin pervaded, suddenly a new ambiance. Madeline looked at her niece, delighted to see her reaction. This was promising, Gillian's expression was a sight to be seen as she accepted the boozy kiss. There was a little shrug as she said to the group, 'This is my aunt.' It was more of a warning than an introduction. 'Lovely,' said the man who was a sailor and he put his arm around Madeline's shoulder. 'We're going to the happy hour,' said the woman, 'Coming? Haven't seen you there for ages.'

Happy Hour! Madeline assumed this was nothing to do with the Salvation Army. Her enquiring glance resulted in an explanation. 'It's a special time in the pub for those who know . . . all drinks are half priced.'

'And we can get a good start,' said the lady in the red coat.

'We're going to the Jazz Club.' Her niece made their venue seem an affectation. 'Oh my,' her tone emphasised the thought. 'Anyway, I'll see you soon.' She jabbed her sailor in his ribs, 'He's only here for the weekend.' Then she re-wound her arms about his frame and they staggered off.

Suddenly all the years between now and her own dockyard days seemed as nothing. Madeline and Gillian looked straight into each other's eyes and smiled . . . there was real understanding.

'New people in my old world,' said the older woman.

Her Place on the Moor

Arnold Cooke kicked his gelding into a faster trot. They were late, he and the Hon. Madeline Carmichael, and he knew the big woman on the Irish bay was a stickler for formality . . . she aimed to be on time. She called over her shoulder, her voice was strident, she might have been out on the moors on a windy day, calling to him across a gorse covert.

'I'm not as young as I was. *Anno domini.* Well it is inevitable and I'll go as far as to admit it in front of certain people. Mind you, I don't expect any of them to agree . . . not out loud. It's not so much the years mounting up as the pounds . . . kilograms as they say these days.'

'As long as they keep the horse measurements in hands,' Arnold said, and she snorted agreement, then continuing, 'Thank God for our British hunters . . . up to plenty of weight and all that . . . and manners to burn. Thank god for a sensible father who made certain of my seat.'

Arnold looked at the ample proportions of his employer and noted how well they matched the strong quarters of her mount. Laughter was far from his mind. He had known her as a child. He accepted the arrogance in her attitude to all those who worked to maintain the estate and the running of the local hunt as he accepted her brusque loyalty to those who depended on her family for their living.

The two riders came to the 'Moorland Maidens'. It was a place avoided by foxes, hounds and horses for a reason no one could supply. A slab of granite lay flat against the slope of the land forming a half-circle and around this were other large rocks, irregular in shape, maintaining the appearance of one unit. The first quick look gave an impression of figures standing around an altar. Arnold was used to the scene now and for him it was merely a group of big stones which meant a swerve towards the sea for the hunting field whenever the hounds ran over this part of the country. On the opposite side of the 'altar' there was a green, luscious patch which was recognised by moorland people as a danger zone. He remembered the time one of the young hounds had veered to this side of the area and had been trapped and how his horse had stepped in the bog as he tried to retrieve it . . . up to the withers in no time. He owed his life to Madeline on that bitter day. Her voice boomed across the moors as she called for help; her arms hung on to him as she shouted to the other riders for help. 'Now Cooke, you keep that gelding's head above the mire. I'll keep hold of you. We'll have you both out in no time.' And they did. He could still hear the sucking pop, like a cork from an ink bottle, which accompanied the emergence of the slime-covered horse and rider. Only three years ago. Arnold could not pass this place without a shudder.

Now they reached a path which led through the banks of dried, stringy heather. The horses, ears pricked, heads lifted, broke into a canter. The breeze came from the south-west and brought a special wet mixture of scents.

'How many times, Cooke? How many times?'

'A good few, Ma'am.'

Once they had ridden along the path on the edge of the cliff they would be able to cut through the Church Road and be on the square. Many people were gathered already. Madeline moved towards the group of red coats as the mounted horses made a path for her.

'Morning, Master.'

'Morning, Ma'am. Looks like we'll have a soaking by the end of the day.'

'I sincerely hope it won't be the last.'

The seasoned features of the Master creased into approval. The landlord came from the ivy-covered doorway of the hotel. He carried the first tray of glasses. Hands reached out for a fair measure of rum punch. Old friends drank in silence. In the square there were sounds of clopping hooves, murmurs of conversation from the spectators and high-pitched from a group of younger members who were having a few rounds in on their own account.

'So that woman bought Charlie's roan after all.' Madeline's voice was envious. 'He reminds me of my Tristan, remember? Carried me for years without a fall until age slowed him.' She sighed. 'I wouldn't take him then. Couldn't bear to think of him back with the tail-end . . . his pride. I couldn't bear it.'

'I suppose it comes to us all,' said the Master.

'I suppose so.'

They sat on their horses and sipped reflectively, two stalwart representatives of the country establishment. They watched as Arnold worked with the huntsman, helping with the hounds and guiding the lorry which had brought them to the back of the car park. The clock showed almost eleven o'clock. Glasses were replaced on trays or put down hurriedly on window sills and the horses collected in readiness for the move. The buzz of conversation faded and, except for an occasional impatient scrape of a hoof, it was quiet. The space around the Master cleared. He was raising the horn to his lips. The big man in hunting pink sat on his seventeen-hand chestnut with dignity as it trotted at the head of the 'field' out towards the moorland cliffs. There was the usual clatter; a few lighthearted bucks and those with any sense let their mounts keep in the centre of the field. Madeline, a founder-member of the committee as she was, had her place just behind the pack. Arnold Cooke was near her. The Hon. Madeline could be carried away once the blood was up. He had to be certain she did not take chances; he would be at hand to help her remount if she needed; he would smooth her path as unobtrusively as he could.

They were strung out now along the very path they had taken on their way to the Meet. The space between the leaders and the rest was widening and those who had hunted this land before guessed they would reach the gorse spinney before the first Draw.

Madeline had jammed her feet home in the stirrups and had buttoned up the collar of her jacket. The wind had freshened and it was pulling against them as they galloped. She had no qualms about the sure-footedness of her mare and was settling her seat-bones deeper into the saddle. The difficulties of the morning's preparation were forgotten, as were the niggling doubts about her decreasing energy. Lately it did take her much longer to prepare things in the morning.

They stopped in the spinney as the pack cast around. In the shelter and because of the close proximity of men and warm horses, steam formed a mist which might have come from the channel. The blonde woman had pushed her way near the Master and Madeline, tolerant of most people's foibles as she was, tightened her lips, even the horses had more manners than some of the new members.

Arnold seemed to be looking nowhere except at the back of the huntsman yet he had noticed the determined set of Madeline's shoulders. Something had rattled the old girl, he thought. He saw the roan which used to belong to Colonel Charles Hawthorne breast his way amongst the leaders. His own tough, weathered face seemed not to change but as his head turned towards Madeline she knew that he understood.

They had a line and the pack, straight as a dye, were on the scent. The field, motionless now, could see a dog running towards the higher ground and the Moorland Maidens. The horn sounded and the chase began, everyone careful to keep from crossing the scent.

The hounds checked and everything was quiet again. Madeline spoke over her shoulder, 'He's done it again, Cooke.' Arnold replied, 'Our secret, Ma'am.' The Master cursed loudly. He did not know that Madeline and Arnold, sworn to secrecy, knew that the fox had slipped into the waters of The Black Pond and was lying, nose on a rock, waiting for his pursuers to leave him in peace.

All this meant a change to the cultivated farmland which lay to the south-east.

Arnold's face was troubled. Steady as Madeline's mare was, it had a fair turn of speed and, over the walls, his own mount would not be able to keep her in sight as he would like and knew, at times, was necessary. The rain which had threatened began to fall.

'Super,' said the blonde. 'Now we can try you, my lad.'

'Super,' Madeline who had heard, mimicked with scorn. Only those who were riding near them noticed.

Another cast about and a second scent was taken. The roan was edging Madeline's mare to the side with selfish cunning, the blonde had chosen her route over the lowest part of the wall. The missing stones at this point gave her at least a foot advantage. Arnold tried to move on to Madeline's right side. Braving her country gift of withering rhetoric, he tried to force her sideways so that she would have to follow the roan over the dip in the wall. She shot him a glance from under her grey bushy eyebrows which contained more amusement than anger. She reined in so that he was bound to move forward and out of her path.

Then, with her black boots pressed into the sides of her mount, she went forward to the unbroken part of the granite wall. Arnold was landing on the other side when he saw the riderless mare gallop off in front of him. Before the first cries of 'Loose horse' he had dismounted and was kneeling beside the inert figure of his mistress.

Her eyes opened and looked directly into his. Arnold, in all the years, had never seen Madeline's face at such close quarters. The eyes were deep and beautiful almost, in a crumpled mass of face. 'My damn neck.' These were the last words she spoke.

On the following Tuesday, the members of the hunt committee rode with somber pageantry towards Moorland Maidens. The Master led her bay Irish mare which was draped in the Carmichael colours and the Vicar, horseman himself, carried the urn which contained her ashes. These were scattered with ancient pagan ceremony on the flat 'altar' stone. The Master played 'Gone Away', the notes of the horn plaintive in the winter afternoon. The Vicar voiced the thought which must have been in the minds of many who were present, that Madeline must surely have been with them. 'A woman who knew her place.' All would agree.

They rode back in silence – her mare might have trained all her equine life for such a ceremonial occasion. It was the end, also, Arnold realised, of his own hunting days. There was no more need to protect anyone and it was impossible to visualise riding without his mistress.

Because Madeline would have wished it so, the hunt met as usual on the following Saturday. The field was not as exuberant as usual and Arnold followed on foot as they made for the Moorland Maidens.

He was glad he saw it with his own eyes, it would have been almost impossible to believe. But for the first time in the history of the hunt, the hounds led the field right through the Moorland Maidens and over the big flat stone.

Still Waters

The dazzle of a wide river mouth blurred and was lost in the tree-lined land. Here, under low branches, water dulled and receded. It was a dark mirror and reflected grotesque human forms, elongated oars and cloudy shadows of foliage. On its surface, thick bundles of boot-lace floated, strips of dangerous seaweed, ready to trap unwary bathers.

There was the narrow strip of light which meant open sea. To the west, the river flowed against the ancient walls of Falmouth harbour. The harbour with its confusion of old warehouses; dominated by the sturdy funnels of oil-tankers or rusty liners in for a face lift, but it was decorated with colourful sailing craft. These glided among their ocean-going sisters. From this scene came the hammer sounds, hooters to mark ends of shifts and at times, the hiss of steam.

They were out now, past the lighthouse, beyond Castle Point and almost out in the open sea.

'Ease off, Pete,' Raymond said to his son.

There was no need for words. Already the throb of the engine had died, the speed of the boat checked until it held its own, just, against the moderate swell of waves.

Pete's eyes swept the horizon. He noted a few boats lying over to the west. Automatically he steered towards them.

The two mackerel lines were out already. Madge held one and Sally the other. Madge, Raymond's sister, Sally's aunt, an older version of Sally, was back for her holiday. Pete studied them both, so alike, and remembered one very young moment of his when his aunt's husband had died, and he had said he would

127

marry her when he was older. Everyone had laughed then, yet the words had comforted Madge.

Those sincere words, wrested from him at an impressionable age when he had seen his normally laughing, lively aunt broken by grief, crying against the severity of the blow, were now forgotten. By everyone but him, he supposed. He still squirmed as he remembered. What a sentimental idiot she must have thought him.

Madge did not think that. The words at the time had comforted her and forever, as she looked at him, her eyes would soften. Gentle Pete, she would think . . . too gentle maybe. I hope life deals kindly with him.

Now, as she sat alongside Sally, that time was long past. She had adjusted and her life was crammed with excitement and incident. She had her job and her interests. Life was almost too full. At the moment, she revelled in the utter waste of hours as the rush of city hustle ebbed into the background of her mind. Her hands twined around the taut cord.

'This is marvellous,' she cried, 'If I were only living here again I'd be an addict . . . a regular member of your crew.'

The words were addressed to Raymond who looked pleased. He nodded with instant understanding.

'It gets to you,' he said, 'this is how I unwind. Out here late on a summer's evening the office seems very far away.' He gave a dry look towards his son. 'That and Pete's incessant chatter.'

Everyone laughed. Pete's brown eyes screwed faintly in response to the joke. Raymond continued, 'The other night, the only speech we got out of him was, "Isn't it about tea time?"'

There was a slight tug on Sally's line. Quickly it was pulled in. Another mackerel thrown into the blood-spattered box to thresh in whatever fishy death-agonies fate had decreed.

The engine chugged. Now the swell was harder. Slaps under the keel told more than the full sails of other craft that the wind was freshening.

Pete's lean face betrayed little interest. His hands moved with automatic reflex which came from hours of experience . . . now to the right, now to the left, as he guided the boat over good pollock ground. Once he had a longing to join in the general talk but he could never think of witty remarks. However, lately he had made a thing about his reticence. Other people teased him about it and they accepted it, now it was his own. It was part of his personality.

Raymond took Sally's line. His hands were quick and deft as he changed it for a longer one. He intended to fish more deeply.

'There,' he told her, 'You won't find this so easy. One good bass and we can all go home.' He leant back a little and flung the line clear of the boat and out into the waves. He met female eyes and countered their admiration with, 'I know where they live.'

Pete's eyes were still fixed on the width of the river mouth. He had not heard Raymond's words. He was thinking of the Sailing Club dance held on the previous night.

The fair-haired girl in a soft white dress had laughed when they had both jumped out of the way of a man carrying a tray of drinks. Then she had taken a second look at him, stared into his eyes with a sudden wondering look. He closed his mind against the sea now and heard the saxophone taking the lead in the small band and the song taken up by a young fellow at the microphone. The rest of the musicians were low in the background. She had smelt like honeysuckle on a hot day and, as they stayed close to each other, he felt her warmth. The tray had been righted and those around them had cleared away, but they remained together. His legs were like lead, rooted. He could not move. He waited for her to go, yet she stayed near and the music changed. He tried to find words and, for the first time in ages, he wished for the slick tongue of friends or the easy wit of his father. There was no credit in this silence. The words were poignant in the new song . . . sloppy, sentimental, but they caught at a longing inside him and held there. She came a little nearer with a lifting of her arms, then they were together, swaying with slowness in time to the music. Not dancing really, just holding . . . and the group had played a kind of slow jazz, not a bit like their usual hectic beat. She was quiet too and he knew she was as moved as he was. He watched her smooth, freckled skin and saw the little smile on her lips. Then her eyes looked up towards his and they were glimmering with a kind of laughing promise. He felt her body against his own frame and would remember forever the softness. The feel of her in his arms was as if he had found something that was to be his own and he could not relate it to his first sight of the sophisticated sun-burnt girl in a slim white dress.

Madge had gone into the cabin to pour out tea. Sally's slim elegant hand was on the line now, quiet and assured. Pete glanced at his sister and looked away. They had been such friends but, at the moment her clean limbs seemed to emphasise just how little he knew of real womanhood. He had seen her change from a boyish hoyden into an attractive girl. Her brown hair and large sparkling eyes emphasised the small face, clear of make-up. He thought of the whiter femininity of his blonde, tried to picture her on the boat . . . and failed. This is all right for old men and kids, he thought . . . dismissing the times he had chugged through the rain, autumn gales, or lingered on summer after-noons until evening and dark. How he had filled himself with dreams and thoughts of the sea, basing his whole outlook and purpose on the wishes of his father. To be like his father. No . . . he could never be like him. He could never hold down a busi-ness or grip an audience, or amuse his friends as his father could. At most, he could fulfil his father's dream of an affinity between his son and the sea. He could realise that ambition by joining the navy. It had been their mutual dream.

That was until Saturday night when he held Maria close to his heart.

Sally ceased humming and started pulling the line back to the boat. Her small hands worked with efficient energy. Madge had come out of the cabin ready to serve out mugs of tea. Raymond was standing ready to take the fish off the hook. He leant and grasped the struggling mackerel when it was landed. He freed the hook expertly from its mouth and flung it with some scorn into the box.

'Poor little thing,' said Sally, 'Just because it isn't a bass.' She watched it struggle for a moment, then turned her bright brown face towards the sea, paying out her line, little by little. Already her mind had forgotten.

'That's just it,' thought Pete. 'Sally doesn't care about life or death, not really. Maria could never bear to catch a fish.'

Slapping and rocking, the boat moved nearer the lighthouse. Pete remained quiet. He was hearing the wailing sounds of his Saturday world and was wondering where and how he could learn to dance well enough to be confident. He wished he was suave and ten years older. Suddenly, his eyes met the blue ones of his aunt. His glance would have swept past her towards Castle Point, but she looked at him intently. Her eyes studied him, the gangling boy, through to the young tumult which was stirring inside him.

'Pete won't want to spend his Sundays like this much longer.'

Raymond turned with a swift movement of his shoulders towards his son and frowned. Pete noted his expression with a slight shock. A flash of understanding swept his dependence on his father away forever. He could see in Raymond's eyes the sudden terror, the picture of lonely nights on the little craft without the companionable silence of his son. Quiet, scraping homecomings. No one to moor his boat or help string the catch or to hang on to every word he uttered. And Raymond saw the autumn of his own life, motor trips to the edge of the shore, binoculars sweeping the horizon, the witch sounds of the gulls which told why the ships were manoeuvring around the lighthouse.

Pete looked down. Maybe he'd want to go out still, sometimes, just for old time's sake. But, after all, the old boy couldn't depend on him for ever. Maybe when he and Maria were married . . . but by then they'd have their own children.

While the Tide Comes In

Along Swansea sands the sea never intruded. When it was low tide the sands stretched and emptied into nothingness. When the tide was high, it washed over the sands in grey anonymity. Afterwards I never remembered what the tide looked like when it was in, but always I could remember the flat, yellowy-brown sand-fields when it was out. The dogs running for sticks and elderly men with hands behind their backs who paced a daily dozen steps towards the sea.

Brian and I ran most days. It was the space, nothing to stop the wind and the secret of nowhere.

We would walk down a concrete path away from the triangled green outside the Brangwyn and the rearing new flats or terraced houses which were steep against the sides of Town Hill. We would leave the people behind; the wives with shopping baskets, men moving from one office to another, nurses coming or going to the hospital; some holidaymakers with faces browned by the Gower winds. Here would be our world. Only people like us left the pavements and the streets. Those who were not yet caught in the shuffling rustle of a morning.

Brian was walking carefully. I knew that every grain of sand which collected on the edge of his shoes was making him more angry, angry with me. He had wanted to be up there today . . . today he was strung taut to play his note in the upward medley of noise on the streets; taut . . . in his dark, narrow suit and clear just-look-how-an-executive-should look collar . . . tuned to make the right sounds to impress the interviewing head of a firm.

I had insisted. Ever since the first minute of the day when I had seen the excitement in his face about a prospect of a future which did not include me.

I was kicking the sand and moving round him in circles. I saw the sand as a big stage and I was a ballet dancer trying to lure a prince into the watery depths of my kingdom. Only my prince wasn't looking. His face was dark; his thoughts were centred on a kingdom of his own; reigned by himself, a young tycoon launching out with brash, new ideas in the world of global marketing. If he were old enough I could have loved him; if he were old enough to be attentive; old enough to be strong; old enough for me to follow him. But he was thin and young and his fair hair was flowing ridiculously in the wind coming from the sea. And I had made him come.

'No,' he had said, 'not now. Not before the interview.' He was pompous and dressed like a grey raven.

'Why ever not? We always do. It might be our last time.' I was cunning. Not for a moment did I think it would be the last time. He said, 'So what!' Just like that. He did not care. All he thought about was getting a tin-pot job and going away. He wouldn't remember anything and all the time he thought I should understand.

I saw the women with their shopping baskets and the men about their business and I saw Brian becoming a part of them already. We faced each other stiff and aggressive, daring each other to say goodbye. I said, 'If I had known this, I wouldn't have come. You said you wanted me . . .'

Brian looked at me. His eyes told me this was true but his words, 'I thought you would want to come. It doesn't matter . . . not to me.'

'Come on the sands like we always do. Maybe I'll bring you luck.' I was saying anything just to make him do this thing for me. He sighed and I added a note of pleading, 'For the last time.'

And here we were. But if he had loved me he would be telling me his thoughts; about the new job. Where would we go? He wasn't saying anything.

The sea skulked in the distance. There was nothing to see, only a long stretch all the way to the beginning of the docks. I stopped weaving and pirouetting and walked beside him, just as silent. I was thinking how lucky I had found all this about him in time. He could go as far away as he liked.

We separated the moment we had come together on the sands. Life with him would be as endless as this walk and only up there, among the shops and houses there would be life and movement.

When we came to the arch at the bottom of Wind Street, I thought: 'In the darkness of the tunnel he will kiss me . . . like he always does and everything will be all right again.' But he kept trudging on, not seeing me or anything else except the shadows in his mind.

We went to our coffee bar. Walking up the wide, busy street from the docks; passing the brass and wooden windows, the tobacconists with fancy packets, Turkish cocktail, Passing Cloud, warm smells from Havana; the Expresso bars; the mullioned panes of the wine shop; the alleys between the vaults, smelling of beer and Salubrious Passage. We walked on the pavements that were Swansea and which had known all sorts of foreign feet and spilt blood or wine and broken glass.

This walk past the barrels rolling from lorries into the secret doorways and people moving in and out of the banks and the Post Office and workmen shouting; cars moving all the time and hardly any women because Wind Street is a man's street. The ruins of the castle behind the *Evening Post* office was seen. I saw it in a new light at this time. At last we were in the light and space of the lawns and civic flowers outside Sidney Heath's.

Brian combed his hair and wiped the sand from his shoes. He was feeling better. He began to talk, 'You realise this will be for

135

both of us, don't you? If I could only get in . . . I know I can do well. Jobs aren't so easy to get . . . good jobs . . . even with a degree. There are so many of us.'

I thought he was young and there was plenty of time. If he loved me he would not be in such a hurry to go. And I could love him. I knew that, once he had grown up.

In the café Vincent Jones was home on holiday. He told me: 'What a change . . . now I see a lovely woman.' When I had seen him last he was in college and I was in the fifth form. He wouldn't have noticed me in those days . . . I like best being called a woman. It was the first time. It put me on a different level from Brian, who was a boy. In spite of his interview and his new career.

My body became liquid and I assumed a mysterious air of silence. I smiled wanly at Brian who was now beginning to talk like mad. 'You sound nervous.' I meant to sound consoling but Brian thought otherwise. 'Don't patronise me.' I looked towards Vincent and shrugged, 'You see what I mean.'

Brian kept looking at his watch. When it was a quarter past eleven he stood up. He looked at me. Now there was no Vincent, just the two of us. Brian was young and defenceless. I wanted to give him some of my own confidence. 'This is it,' he said. 'Well, good luck then.' He kept looking at me as if he knew I wanted him to be O.K. I was quiet . . . 'Well, I'll see you.' I replied, 'I'll wait.'

He walked out of the café, stopping at the counter near the door to pay. For a second, as he was taking the money out of his trouser pocket he looked like a man . . . a boy pretending. My eyes began to feel warm, if I blinked I was sure there would have been a tear.

Vincent was still there but during the last few minutes he had gone flat. He was just a big square. I wanted him to go so that I would be on my own when Brian came back. Vincent said, 'The Surf Boys are in the Top Rank on Friday.'

'Oh yes.'

'Maybe I'll see you.' I shook my head. I sat, not speaking, waiting for him to go. I heard his chair scrape and he stood up. He was looking down, puzzled and a little younger. 'Ta ta, then,' he said and was gone.

When the glass door on to the street had closed behind him I looked up and ordered another coffee. Ten minutes had gone; another half hour perhaps and Brian would be back. I watched the girl behind the counter, just my age, mouthing a message to two boys on the other side of the street. Her hair was dry and brushed like fine brass wire.

Three people came in, drank coffee and went out. The door opened just when my head was turned away. I felt as if I had missed someone when meeting him from a train. Brian came over to the table. His face was strained. I had never seen him look so sad.

Suddenly I knew what loving was. Love was being big and warm and giving. I wanted to cradle my arms around Brian and comfort him. So he hadn't got their rotten job. What did it matter. There were other chances and he was young and clever and he would get somewhere someday . . . whatever they did to him. I said, 'I'll get the coffee.'

When I came back, I said, 'Did you want a sandwich? I got some, just in case.'

He was looking at me as if he had never seen me before. 'I'll have to go away, you know, just for a while. But if you could wait . . . just a little, the salary will be good, we'll probably . . .'

I looked at him and felt the thrill of his success. 'Brian love . . .' I said and his eyes began to smile into mine . . . 'That's great.'

Tale of the Green Sea Witch

We were out past the Manacles. The sky was darkening and the wind was coming from the south. Strange how the voice of the wind changes! It whines and the sound carries the desolation of snow deserts, moans with the bleakness of cold, swirling waters. It echoed the howl of starving wolves.

It was time to make for home. Already the bell on Black Rock had tolled its warning and the sombre note reminded of past, savage storms. We set the boat for safer waters inland, the three of us, Jim, my brother, Peter, who came to crew for us and myself. I had argued with my stepmother until she allowed me to go on this trip. She said I was just as wild as everyone said I was.

What was being wild? No one explains because they do not understand. I know that since I could remember I was part of the shingle and the rocks. I felt the colours and moods of the sea and the different sounds of the wind. The feel of a boat was just like the feel of my own legs and arms.

All of us were used to the Channel and these lethal rocks. We knew how far we could go.

And on the boat things were going well. The engine chugged strongly as we left the area of danger and we were all relieved that we had made it in time. The slap of the waves against the side of the boat became more gentle. We allowed thoughts of warm drinks and roaring, kitchen stoves to cheer the last moments of the journey.

We approached one of the tentacles known as Long Reef. It curved round the inlet, forming a sort of natural harbour. Once we passed this we were as good as home.

We came nearer the end of Long Reef. It was the best sight in the world and all of us were staring at its familiar outline. Then we saw it! It seemed to be an animal at first which came out from the sea to rest on the rocks. We came as close as we dared because it might be a seal. Seals were found sometimes in this area when the sea was rough.

We drew nearer until we heard a voice. It was unlike any human voice but neither was it like an animal or bird. It was haunting and sad like a sea shanty sung by a grieving boy; each word was penetrating and we were mesmerised. I could feel the throbbing as my heart beat. Each one of us heard it. Our breath was held as if to listen more, or, maybe not to be heard, but the sound surrounded us completely. Closer still, we saw it was more human than anything else. The colour of the skin was like moonlight. That was what struck us most, the colour of the skin, standing out like phosphorus against the darkened cliffs. The water in the shadow of the rocks was already black. There was no moon and only the lights from the village showed, not enough to make any difference.

The boat began moving towards the rock. Peter was steering while Jim and I stood by the engine. We did not speak to each other, yet the boat drew nearer. Peter, it was, who spoke first, 'We can't just pass . . . can we? I mean, we've got to see what it is.' Peter had to know the ins and outs of everything, curious, not to learn to get wiser but just so that he could put it out of his mind.

Jim was silent and I knew his mind had returned through the years to a sunlit moment on the quay.

He was a boy, playing with other children. The old men were leaning on the sea wall, looking out, for it was in this way they spent their time. Looking out at sea and feeling the rounded warmth of the wall against their bodies. They would tell their stories over and over again. Once they began the children stopped to listen because when the men relived their experiences and adventures children's games were tame and insipid.

The old men talked, touching once more the stiff wet ropes on bleached scrubbed boards under a distant sun; they tasted salt and felt the singing wind around their ears. And they were strong and young.

Jim had this far-away look and I knew what he was thinking. I watched his face as he remembered. Like him I was hearing the story we had heard so often. My grandfather's story about a green woman who came out of the sea to sit on the end of the reef when some watery disaster was imminent.

My grandfather told of how men had seen her the night before the famous *Queen Marguerite* was wrecked; the night he himself was washed up, locked in the dead, stiff arms of a young man of, apparently, great wealth. Nobody else was said to say anything. Only Old Mother Pascoe who lived to be over a hundred years old remembered how the rings were cut off the drowned man's fingers and the boy was brought up with a fisherman's family in the village. The rings were sold but the garnet ring which was on a chain around my grandfather's neck was not taken. He kept it always.

Even I remember Old Mother Pascoe. She lived at the back of the cottages on the harbour front, the ones with thatched roofs with almost always open doors. There was a wide, cobbled path, broken by shallow steps which led to them so that it was easy to run down to the quay whenever there were tea leaves or fish guts or slops to be thrown over to the waiting gulls . . . when the tide was high of course. Old Mother Pascoe wore long, black skirts and screamed orders at everyone. She did not have any teeth and Jim was terrified of her. In the evenings, sitting on the wooden bench, she would talk to the young wives as they leant against their doorposts and told them about the old days. It was she who described the terrible night when grandfather was saved.

How they set fire to furze and tar barrels on the cliffs to give light. We would be too excited on those long summer nights to sleep and we would hang out of our bedroom windows to listen. We would not join in . . . but gasps or exclamations would draw the rebuke 'get to bed you young night crows.' We listened as the darkness crept over the bay and the smell of pilchards marinating in the night ovens flavoured the air. We heard in the evening the throb of an outgoing fishing boat; a man's shout as he tied up or the sudden quiet as the engine of an incoming trawler cut.

We heard how the tale of the green sea witch had impressed grandfather. He spent many hours watching the reef. Daylight hours and moonlight hours were spent. He saw her once himself and he said, 'Her hair was like seaweed but her face and body showed she was a woman.' He could see only the green glow around her form but even at a distance he felt the impact of beauty. The villagers believed him because he had grown from a dark strong boy to a man with a reputation for courage and intelligence.

Legends grew round the Sea Witch as weeds grew around a tide-washed stone. She became, in spite of her beauty, a sinister omen. Especially when, soon after my grandfather spoke of her, the body of a woman was seen floating amongst the flotsam in the inlet near the reef, her upturned face showed it was the body of his daughter, my mother.

Jim came back from the past and looked at me. He understood that I too had remembered. He looked and his eyes were pleading, 'You tell Peter,' he seemed to say, 'don't let it be me . . . not this time. You tell him he's got to steer the boat away . . . back into the open sea . . . to take our chance.'

I thought, back into the open sea. Back into the tearing force we had just escaped. Just because Jim was afraid to go close to the woman or to admit to his fear. It was madness.

The bell tolled as though it was part of my thought. I could not bring myself to speak. I looked at Jim and shook my head . . . denying him. He wanted me to break the spell but I kept silent. I thought like Peter, my curiosity overcame fear. I shared his overwhelming need to draw close and to see the face of the spirit.

Before Jim spoke, he flashed one look of hate in my direction. I knew it was the accumulated frustrations of our childhoods. The times he had been told, 'Go on, don't be afraid . . . look . . . your little sister does not mind.' The time that I had been given grandfather's ring because I had crewed for him on Regatta Day.

Then, because I loved him and I saw how much it mattered, I forgot everything else but him. I was protective towards him, my elder brother who was almost my child. I opened my lips to say 'Turn back' but Jim had spoke first. 'Yes . . . yes,' I agreed, too late, 'let's get away. Turn out to sea again.'

'To sea. But the bell.' Even Peter's curiosity was subdued at the prospect of a wild open sea. 'We've got to get to shore.'

However, he was beginning to turn. Reluctantly, it seemed the boat moved in a circle away from the inlet near the reef.

Jim's eyes wavered from mine. He knew the truth he had exposed could not be buried quickly. The boat was heading out where the sea shone blood red. The dangerous triangle of light shown by the beam of St Anthony Lighthouse through crimson glass. Blood red the fishermen say, because of the drowned souls from ships which have been hurled against the Manacles.

We lost the sound of the voice in the wind which was waiting for us out in the unsheltered channel. But the last notes were mocking: laughing, as if to say we could not escape from her.

The Sea Witch was wrong. I returned to tell our tale.

* * *

I remembered what happened right up until the moment we were thrown into the sea. A wave caught us in a powerful swirl, our boat rode in its curve and was tossed upside down in the foaming cataract crest. Peter disappeared immediately but for a long while Jim and I clung together in the waves whilst we were lashed by the splintered timbers of our boat. I remembered the stark agony when Jim's hold began to slacken and his head sank back into the grey depths. Loneliness; regret for the times I might have comforted him and did not; regret for the wonder of life. I remembered the salt-choking water and the cold which froze my breathing into tight iron bands.

Then there was the desperate reach towards a piece of hull, larger than the rest, and my last conscious memory was the garnet ring on my finger. My grandfather's ring.

There were no more memories, for they drowned in a clear greenness of insensibility. The sea was a woman whose arms enveloped me and I was glad. Floating in the mists of twilight was the face of a beautiful woman whose hair was seaweed. Surrounding was the sound of a voice that was haunting and mesmerising, that was not human nor animal. There was a soothing warmth and the sea water was a bath of honey and wine. I floated through the jade pillars of the ocean. There were misty objects, jewelled, set with red garnets, floating within my reach. There were the solid gates of some underwater palace which opened for me to enter. There was a spinning, dizzy lightness which made me part of the phosphorescent water tracks.

The next thing I saw was my hand with its red band and I was fighting the arms which tried to drag me out of my wet heaven. The choking returned and the sea water was pressed out of my resisting body.

*   *   *

All this I remember tonight when I am in my small sitting room. A seaman's wife is often alone and because the moon is high and there are not many good fishing nights left before winter sets in, my husband is out in the boat. He had taken a while to decide because the wind was freshening from the south and he knows how I hate the wind. But even in a harbour cottage now, life is comfortable. I say this though I think often of the past, gossipy days when we were not isolated in our rooms with a television link to another world which is not anything to do with us.

I know I would change my aerial and electric wire any day for the warm communication of Old Mother Pascoe.

It is late and I am lulled by the warmth of the room into a state of drowsiness. My limbs are heavy and when the last flicker from the screen fades, I am too warm and comfortable to cross the room to switch it off.

While I am summoning my energies there is a phosphorescent glow on the screen and the sound of music. Music that is haunting and chilling which mesmerises me into stillness. The glow takes the form of a green woman; her hair is like seaweed and her face should be beautiful but it is twisted in mockery.

Her eyes are looking straight into mine and she is laughing.